"Not that the story need be long, but it
will take a long while to make it short."

— Henry David Thoreau

The Tattooed Woman

Marian Engel was born in Toronto and grew up in various Ontario
towns. She attended McMaster and McGill Universities. Her first
novel, *No Clouds of Glory*, was published in 1968, followed by *The
Honeyman Festival*, 1970, *Bear*, 1976 (which won the Governor-
General's Award), *The Glassy Sea*, 1978 and *Lunatic Villas*, 1981. She
was the first chairman of the Writers' Union of Canada and was ap-
pointed an Officer of the Order of Canada in 1982.

She died at age 51 in Toronto in 1985. *The Tattooed Woman* is Marian
Engel's last published work.

1986
Nov.

To Barbara,
Mazaltov on
Robin's safe
arrival!

from
Lola + Elaine
+ NCJW of Canada's
Book club

THE TATTOOED WOMAN

Marian Engel

With a Preface by Timothy Findley

Penguin Books

Penguin Books Canada Ltd., 2801 John Street, Markham, Ontario, Canada L3R 1B4
Penguin Books Ltd., Harmondsworth, Middlesex, England
Penguin Books, 40 West 23rd Street, New York, New York 10010 U.S.A.
Penguin Books Australia Ltd., Ringwood, Victoria, Australia
Penguin Books (N.Z.) Ltd., Private Bag, Takapuna, Auckland 9, New Zealand

First published by Penguin Books Canada Ltd., 1985

Typesetting by Jay Tee Graphics Ltd.
Manufactured in Canada by Gagne Printing Limited

Canadian Cataloguing in Publication Data

Engel Marian, 1933-1985.
The tattooed woman

(Penguin short fiction)
ISBN 0-14-008115-1

I. Title. II. Series.

PS8559.N44T37 1985   C813'.54   C85-098540-4
PR9199.3.E5T37 1985

Contents

Acknowledgements

Some of these stories have appeared previously:

"The Tattooed Woman" on *Anthology,* 1975;

"The Last Wife" as "Last Happy Wife" in *Chatelaine,* 1977;

"Madame Hortensia, Equilibriste" in *Saturday Night,* 1977;

"The Life of Bernard Orge" on *Anthology,* 1980;

"Feet" in *Quest,* 1981;

"Anita's Dance" in *Chatelaine,* 1981;

"The Smell of Sulphur" on *Anthology,* 1983;

"Banana Flies" in *Women and Words,* 1983;

"Could I Have Found A Better Love Than You?" as "Under the Hill" in *Room of One's Own,* 1984;

"Gemini, Gemino" on *Anthology,* 1985.

Marian Engel and
The Tattooed Woman
Timothy Findley

In the end, it is all behind us: the thinking and the making, the doing and the writing. The drawing of lines — of final lines — is inevitable. And so, though Marian Engel is only recently dead as this is being written, it hardly seems the right tack to take — the tack which dwells on death — as if death were any good reason to publish a book. This book was planned before she died. And it caused a good deal of planning, a very good deal of excitement and not a little bewilderment. "Which stories shall they be?" she would ask us over and over. "Do you think there should be a unity — or shall I just throw in every story I like, a sort of *grab bag*?"

Much of the time the book was being planned, Marian Engel was bedridden: sometimes in hospitals, sometimes at home. The coming and the going between one place and the other became a kind of routine. The walls of my kitchen are still plastered with pieces of paper reading: *Marian — Rm 414* and then a telephone number. Also *M. home Tuesday, 3:00 p.m.* Back and forth and back again. And the stories went with her — sometimes piles of them — sometimes just a shopping bag with one or two or three. Whichever bed she currently occupied would have all these pages beside it or spread out over the covers — though there wasn't much room on the covers: Marian liked very much to occupy as much of the covers as she could with her own arms and legs. She was a great one for sprawling — like a child with toys — except the toys were her stories.

"Which, which, which?" she would ask — and she would ask everyone. But, even while she was asking, you could tell she wasn't paying the slightest attention to your answers. She already had her answers. She knew perfectly well which stories she wanted to include. The asking of the question was just a diversionary tactic. *Maybe if I ask for their opinion, they'll leave me alone to do my choosing.* You could tell this, because when you did give an answer, somehow she would counter it: "No. I've already decided against that one. . . ." Or: "Do you *really* like that one. Really?" The implication here was: *what peculiar taste you have.*

You learned fairly quickly to shut up.

Some of the stories couldn't be found. They were deep in boxes or deeper still in Robert Weaver's filing system at the CBC. Others had to be sent from her agent in New York. Some were hiding under her bed. Neatly, I might add. Hiding there neatly.

Ultimately, she made the choice of "unity." The stories have a collective "oddness." But "oddness" is a word you must be careful of. Marian Engel's sense of oddness is very often one of mere apartness. Her people lived apart, making their peace with life and what passed for life, with a kind of wonderful valour. She never gave them short shrift: she never short changed them; she never demeaned them.

The great wonder is the way they went about their lives, working out their problems as if what they were doing was ordinary and everyday. But, of course, it wasn't. A person does not, as a rule, for instance, decide to draw attention to herself when she feels her husband leaving her, by scarring herself with razor blades. But, in Marian Engel's hands, this woman with the scars becomes a marvel of self control. Her scars become works of art: *she* becomes a work of art. And it is that facet of Engel's imagination that sets her people apart from all the other people in fiction. She could show you their hurt in ways that you would never forget. Cannot forget. And won't because — like the Tattooed Woman herself — the scars she makes are as much on you as on herself. But, when you come away from her, you have not been disfigured — just transformed.

Timothy Findley
Cannington, Ontario
March 1985

Introduction

My short story sits like a Magic Bicycle Kit on the front lawn. Actually, it is an Instant War Memorial. It is in a brown wooden crate and the parts are packed in excelsior. I have checked to see that they are all there. The weather is beautiful: a small wind, high in the sky; the trees putting out the tenderest of their green leaves. No excuse to put the construction off.

No desire, either. The front lawn is literally the size of a bedsheet and must be cleared before a large, ugly brown square is left on its thin grass. I could work on my novel, which is always there in the background, nagging, but the fact is that the story must be put together in order to feed us all while the novel, which can't hope to produce income for another year, is being completed. Besides, I like the job.

The trouble is, I haven't got the right tools, I can't buy them, I am forced to sit here through fair weather and foul, suitable times and untenable, until I can spew them up from some inner region which obeys no rules in the matter. For twenty years I tried to invent those tools and now that I have access to the Soft Spanner and the Hysterical Wrench, Faulkner's Torque Assembly and Laurence's Pearline Drill, they've started playing games with me. They hide, I seek, they reveal themselves when they please. It's not fair, it's not logical. I want my Instant War Memorial, I need my Instant War Memorial, I will have it.

But not when I want it.

I can dance with rage, but it won't do any good. My inner voice has to whisper through, "Have you thought of marrying the logical person?" There it is: the connection. I think of my daughter, who rejected irregular verbs until she was twelve.

I don't believe in ghosts and fairies, except of course for the Knockers, the Jewish fairies in the Cornish tin mines, but I have been made to believe in the irrational, the area where, when the skin of logic is pulled back, anything can happen. Perhaps that is why I attract people who have found the Holy Grail.

For a long time I wrote short stories as practical exercises in earning necessities, chronicles to pay the bills. They did what they were told to do and failed to be any kind of art. Then irrationality decided to creep in, and the richness that comes from having written for long enough to know it is no use holding anything back. Robert Weaver, who will remain in history as the man who has done most for Canadian writing, particularly in the line of the short story, began to buy these irrational stories for his CBC radio program Anthology. It became easier to write them because he is the ideal reader: ready for anything but sloppy work.

I am not good at traditional narrative. Reality brings out the worst in me. I have tried and failed to lead a conventional life. When I try to be like other people, I fall out of bed. I wish it were otherwise, I wish I had started from zero, an ordinary Canadian child in an ordinary family with her own house and her own bed, so that ordinary kitchen sinks wouldn't still be magic to me. But then I'd have missed my Heath Robinson childhood, and every morning wouldn't be Christmas.

Ordinary reality keeps turning on me. What I have to deal with is super-reality, that element in everyday life where the surreal shows itself without turning French on us, and people have extraordinary conversations because they have confused clam and lamb soup. I sit in restaurants sometimes and take down their tête-à-têtes, but they never turn out to be like other peoples'. Audrey Thomas has a story called "Initram" in which two writers discuss the conversion of their unhappiness into fiction. My fiction goes at it the other way around: it does things to me.

I have to get out the tools, I have to tackle that kit. The inner impulse that forces me to the typewriter is now aligned with the force that created or found the materials. In a moment, the story will leap out of my arms like a hyperactive baby.

A good story comes from a single impulse, a feeling that can be extended and then encapsulated. Often, in my work, it is an absurd feeling that one isn't there in the mirror, that an abandoned salt mine must be made love in before it is filled with oil, that one's body incorporates the three-year-old one used to be, that life is a tightrope act. If I can make the elements of this feeling cohere and consist, if I can attach them to characters who are instantly believable (for if in the novel you have infinite time and space, in the story you have 18 pages) and images which without being self-conscious give it a shimmer, a gloss (and this is where inner alignment matters), I will have a story. If the parts persist in going their own way, gulping down huge draughts of time, I have the outline of a novel on my hands.

More and more, the irrational, the magical impulse, dominates my work. When the mirror cracks I find the compression necessary to miniaturize the narrative drawl, create a world in small compass.

Many of the stories here were written for Robert Weaver. Others emerged from a well-disciplined Ontario subconscious that knows the ultimate virtue is in paying one's bills. They were sifted through the tattered screen of fine courses on the history of the short story from Constance Beresford-Howe, who thirty years ago assigned me papers on Elizabeth

Bowen and Jean Stafford which gave me great joy, and on the history of English prose from Hugh MacLennan, whose statement ''the best writing comes from a well-rested subconscious'' has proved to be true, as well as the excuse for innumerable dreams. And I put in all those years at the typewriter. When I find out who dictated the text, I'll let you know, but right now I have to lay out my tools and assemble that kit.

Marian Engel
Toronto, Ontario
January 1985

The Tattooed Woman

The Tattooed Woman

For some time, she knew she had been his mother rather than his wife, so that when he told her about his girl she was not surprised. The words that came to her lips she had heard at Jewish weddings: "Mazel tov," she said. Then, "What's she like?"

They were sitting in their usual chairs. It was evening. She had wondered why he had come home that evening. Usually he was out working late.

"Well," he said, "she's — uh, young."

"How young?"

"Twenty-one." He was very shy about the whole thing.

"What's her name?"

"Uh . . . Linda."

"She works in the store, does she?"

"No." But she knew he was lying.

"Dark? Fair?"

"In between. A bit like you . . . a long time ago."

"What are your plans?"

"I don't know." He seemed miserable now, as if he would like to get up and run away. "I'd like to stay here until we decide."

"Of course, dear."

"I think I'll go out now and count the cash." He fled.

She had taken it with great dignity, she decided, and of course there was no other way. She had almost expected it. Every woman of her age expected it. And she had nothing but habit to offer him, really. She had taken it like a queen, she decided, because her mother had told her when something is hard, pretend you are a queen. She let him go and subsided meekly to her own room. When she noticed her hands were shaking, she took a sleeping pill.

They had been married for twenty-one years. The girl was twenty-one, a year older than their son. She was forty-two, exactly twice the girl's age. She had nothing to offer. She had kept her figure, but her body, transformed by hysterectomy and appendectomy, was not new or neat or pretty. Surgeons were better now, she understood.

They had been married for twenty-one years. They were good at avoiding each other. Their son had left home. She, who had only clerked in a store before she met him, had never gone back to work, except in his store. She filled her days with trivia, belonged to a golf club, gossiped with friends, read magazines. Read books, though, too; trying to keep up with the latest public passions. Something that never interested him.

They had been married twenty-one years. The girl was twenty-one. The girl had the same number of letters in her name as she did. The girl had the same fairish hair that she had had, once. "Where's she from?" she asked him.

"Winnipeg," he said, and blushed. She was from Winnipeg.

That night he announced that he was going on a buying trip to Montreal and would be gone for a week.

They had been married for twenty-one years. The girl was twenty-one. Half her age. There was nothing she could do. She was not even sure there was anything she wanted to do. She had been living with him for so long they did not notice each other any more. The girl would notice him, how he had no hair on his left leg because of a bad case of athlete's foot, how his right ear stuck out further than his left.

Well, she said to herself, he isn't really anybody's catch. He snores. In two years he'll be fifty. I must get out and find a lover.

Though she had no idea how, never having been with anyone but him. It's the pill that's done this to us, she thought: letting all the little girls out of sexual quarantine. Then, what am I missing anyway?

She thought of getting a job and dismissed the idea. He had never wanted her to. It was hard to get on the volunteer lists at the hospitals; you had to be Somebody and the wife of the owner of a drug store is not Somebody. She bought a lot of paperback books about ecology and pretended she was studying something. She would have studied something if her father had let her, but he thought she ought to go out to work.

The days were easy. She got up late and took long, soapy showers, polishing her body, thinking always of the girl's body, young and firm and unscarred. Then she played golf, had a few gins with Biddy and Helen at the club — a real widow and a grass widow — and sometimes ate with one or the other.

It was the nights that were bad. She would dress for bed and sit in her lingerie thinking of the girl's body, the legs that had never had veins pulled out, the privates from which children and miscarriages and later tumours had never been extracted. The humiliations she had never been exposed to. Poor, poor little thing. She thought of her as tight and white and neat and almost hairless, like the oriental women in American G.I. stories.

One night when she was thinking thoughts she had not ever dreamed she would think, she shaved her legs and nicked one leg with a razor. Blood poured. It was a shin she often cut, a bumpy shin left over from an awkward childhood. The blood looked very satisfactory.

She took the blade out of her razor and washed it. She went and sat at her dressing table and turned the mirrored lights on. I am forty-two and she is twenty-one, she thought. Neatly and very lightly, she carved a little star on her forehead. Experience must show, she thought.

Her cheeks were a little bumpy with age now, and she thought of African women in the National Geographic magazine with beautiful slashes in their ebony skins. She made a few little marks and decided she lacked technique. Then she went to bed and slept very, very well.

As the nights progressed, her technique improved, partly because she had to stay away from the club; Bid and Helen were sure to notice something. She carved little stars shaped like A's on her arms, and then got up the courage to make curves.

She did not cut deeply. She was not interested in hurting herself. On her breasts she made lovely arabesques, on her forearms almost unnoticeable cross-hatchings of little houses and trees. They did not show very much, but she knew they were there and was comforted.

The store was in an indoor shopping plaza. Her husband was right to be proud of it. He had started as an ordinary druggist and worked hard. It looked like a large, rich, fashionable chainstore, but in reality, it was all his. It was beside a supermarket and the turnover was large. She had made a point of never going there, because she knew he did not like to have her interfering in his life.

The day after he came home, she went in and bought a box of Kleenex. The cashier wore a badge that said "Maureen." She wandered around again (knowing he was never there at that hour, that the dispensing druggist had no idea who she was) and saw a girl putting bottles of hand lotion on a shelf. Her badge said "Linda."

Without taking a look at anything but her uncreased uniform and long taffy-coloured hair, she retreated to the centre of the plaza, where there was a fountain and a set of handsome benches. (Oh, they had been so happy when he had finally taken this store!) She sat beside a fern, lit a cigarette, and began to watch the closed-circuit television set he had had installed to prevent thievery.

Linda crossed and recrossed the little screen. She was young, and not especially pretty. She walked fairly gracefully in white wooden-soled shoes. She had dark eyes and a serious face — hardly ever smiled. She decided she liked her.

That night he was home. She did not turn the light on over her chair. "Did you have a good time in Montreal?"

"Not too bad?"

"Where did you stay?"

"Chateau Champlain."

"Is she good in bed?"

Irritably, he said, "What a thing to ask," and left the room.

Every day, now, she went to the plaza and sat beside the fern. Once she saw her husband come in and very, very carefully not speak to Linda. She ducked into the supermarket and when she got home cut one of the stars in her forehead just a little deeper.

The next day Linda was on cash. She went straight up and bought a package of cigarettes and some matches. The girl had no reaction. She had a clear complexion and a neat little body under her nylon shift. Rather hairy arms. "Eighty-five," she said, in an undistinguished voice.

Well, I was undistinguished too, she thought.

From behind the fern, she saw her husband go behind the cash counter. He was unloading cigarettes. He ran his hand down the girl's back from shoulder to butt. He used to do that to me, she thought.

It was the only time she ever saw him touch her. Mostly, they worked together in dignified silence. The girl was neat and efficient. She would be, she thought. Well brought up, used to helping her mother in the kitchen, putting things away in the right place. I used to help him in the old store when the baby slept in the back. He was a stickler about the shelves.

She hadn't got sloppy, she was not bad-tempered, she had not lost her figure. Funny, she had simply got older. It didn't seem to matter when men got older.

Every day she watched them from behind the fern. One night he came home and said the living room was dusty. "I've been reading so much,'' she apologized.

''That's funny, you never turn the light on at night.''

''My eyes are tired at night now. I'm reading about animals. How they adapt themselves to nature. It's fascinating.''

''I'm sure it is,'' he said, his mind on other things.

I am an artist, now, she thought, a true artist. My body is my canvas. I am very old, and very beautiful, I am carved like an old shaman, I am an artifact of an old culture, my body is a pictograph from prehistory, it has been used and bent and violated and broken, but I have resisted. I am Somebody.

The following week he found her behind the fern. He took her arm roughly. ''It's contemptible to spy on people,'' he said. ''It's beneath you. I can't help it if I love her, I tell you, I can't help it. It's my age.'' Then he saw her arm and said, ''Oh, my God.''

He took her to some kind of doctor. She tried to explain to him that she was an old, wise woman, and at the same time beautiful and new. He asked her where she had marked herself, and she took off her clothes and showed him. ''You must have loved him very much,'' the doctor said.

She tried to remember. ''I wanted him to be happy,'' she said. ''So I must have loved him. When I was young, I clerked in the store, like Linda. My name has the same number of letters as Linda. I am forty-two and she is twenty-one. She is a year older than my son. She is from Winnipeg and I am from Winnipeg. She has darker eyes and her nose is not as nice as mine. But of course the young ones are very good in bed, they are allowed to have more experience.''

The doctor was very gentle. ''I don't want you to do that any more,'' he said. ''I want you to decide where you want to go and what you want to be.''

''I am myself,'' she said.

''Clearly, that has not been enough to sustain you.''

''No.''

''When the scars are healed,'' he said, ''you will cease your mourning.''

"Will I have to go to hospital? He said I would have to go to hospital, I heard him."

"What do you think of when you are marking yourself?"

"I think, she is clean, she is clear, I broke my body for him, now I break it for her. She is my daughter, she is my other self. In this way, I make her old and wise."

"She does not need to be old and wise. She needs nothing from you. The young, as you said, are different now. There is nothing you can give them."

"Will I have to go to hospital? My aunt Florrie had shock treatments. They whipped them with hoses."

"I doubt if they did. Maybe she felt as if they did. What do you want to do?"

She felt both vacant and free. Finally, she said, "I have never travelled. There are things in the world I want to see. If you have a store, you can't get away for very long. You can't trust anyone, you see. I used to mind the store, once, when he did his buying."

"I don't want you to go to hospital. Your husband will make you unguents that will heal your skin. Then, if you want, you will travel, the way your son is travelling. You will see all the things you have always wanted to see. Perhaps that will make you the old, wise woman you want to be."

Then, suddenly, she knew what she had done and why she had done it. She had done it to get his pity, and pity was not a thing he had to give. He and his girl would not come and rub the healing ointments on her body. They would vacate themselves, they would run away to their private pleasures.

"Look," she said, "send me to some kind of clinic where I can get rid of the worst of the scars."

The doctor seemed surprised.

"He can pay," she said.

"You want money now."

"Yes, first pity, then money. Do you think I'm any different from any other woman?"

"Yes," he said, "in all the years . . ." then stopped. "You should go somewhere hot. It will make a very striking tan."

The Last Wife

The Last Wife

Pat was up on a ladder shoving plaster into the hole in Nick's ceiling when the telephone rang. She had been putting off the job for the longest time, had indeed had an estimate from a plasterer, then decided that six small holes left from the rewiring were something she could handle herself. She was, in fact, enjoying pushing the squishy stuff into the crevices when the telephone summoned her. She felt as if she were back in school, getting the little ones to work off their tensions by manipulating clay. She had procrastinated only to discover plastering was very satisfying: good.

The telephone rang. She got down off the ladder automatically. It might be a job for Chris and goodness knew he needed it. Too late she realized she was leaving three doorknobs and a newel post smeared with white.

She picked up the phone, half amused; glanced at the calendar beside it. "It's twenty years today since I met Marina," she thought. Because it was her birthday.

Twenty years. My God. She felt exactly the same as she had at seven and now she was old enough to have known someone for twenty years.

"Hello?"

It was Marina, of course. Marina, to wish her a happy birthday, if not to acknowledge that it was twenty years since they met at the College of Art. "Pat, happy birthday, how are you, the most terrible thing . . ." Marina, all in a rush, without punctuation even by breath.

"Marina, I'm plastering."

"Plastering, what the hell for, can't you afford a plasterer?"

"Cash flow, dear."

"You get into such ugly words when you go into the same business as your husband. Why don't you go back to painting?"

"Marina, it's drying on the phone."

"Listen, I've got to talk to you, can I phone you back?"

"Half an hour, eh? That's what it'll take me to finish and clean up."

She got a rag in the kitchen and retraced her chipping progress, enjoying the texture of the flaking plaster as she went. They had made so many small changes in this house as they went along that it was half made of Polyfilla. Kids grow up, she thought, you reshape your living quarters. And yourself.

She got up on the ladder again and daubed, scraped, patted. Thought more about Marina, who lived in a fluster, in a rush. From crisis to crisis. Was she always upset because she was an artist, because her life had to contain chaos so she could reshape it in order? In twenty years she had bounced like a tennis ball from style to style, form to form, husband to husband, a rushing torrent. And produced. Her work was perhaps not first-rate but it had energy, colour: it caught and held interest. You could forgive a person who produced good work a lot.

But Marina always made her feel guilty. Here she was peaceful, domestic, still with Chris. Still at home. Other mums went out and worked but she found that if she did, Chris missed half his phone calls, the kids missed their home-made food, and she lacked the energy to juggle so many worlds. Funny, she thought, to feel guilty at leading a life that so obviously contained the Christian virtues that she had been brought up to fulfil. She loved Chris, liked to help him, got on well with him. Was sometimes annoyed at the boys, did too much for them, manipulated their moods. Sometimes she thought the four of them were the last happy family.

Dangerous, that, with what was in the air these days: never be smug. She got down off the ladder, collected her implements, washed them, phoned Marina.

Marina had rushed off.

She loved working with her hands. She chipped the drying plaster off the plastic pail very slowly, thinking, Marina, Marina how you have rushed through life as if you were a bit of glass in a kaleidoscope, and how I have stood still. Is it Michael in jail for cocaine this time, or Jerry making a row over David's visiting arrangements, or your dealer shafting you? Has your crazy sister in Halifax made another impossible demand?

Twenty years. She looked at herself in the mirror. There was a definite sag under her chin. They had once both been girls in plaid skirts and saddle shoes, filling in forms at the College of Art. "Hey, that's my birthday." Then she, the plain stolid one, had flown into Marina's vortex, double-dating, lending pencils, sharing an apartment, moving out because of the lovers.

I wasn't so plain, she thought. I had something. I still have Chris.

She did not, she thought, have Marina's energy. She was not passive, no, there was something stubbornly active still inside her; but she was not fit for the hurly-burly aggressive artist's world. She had settled for a stool in a drawing office, drawing exquisite forms to order. She was not a real artist, not an independent.

Marina phoned again as Pat was putting the dinner in the oven. Michael was in jail; her dealer was ripping her off; her sister in Halifax was in bed with a broken ankle and she was going to leave her there, it was time she learned if you were going to have six kids you found help closer than Toronto. But

Jerry was cool, he was speaking to her again, which helped David; in fact he had even bought a picture at her show. And wasn't it soooooo-per that they had known each other twenty years now and would she come out and celebrate?

"I'm sorry, Marina, but I think Chris and the boys have something planned for tonight."

"Pat, you're so square!"

"Well, it's too late to change now. Do you want to come over for a while?" From your rainbow to my plateau? Marina didn't. She needed her whirl.

Chris and the boys had pink wine and pink roses for her. Chris looked wiped out, too tired. Times are getting tough, she thought. I'm glad the house is paid off. I'm glad I can do my part. He's so hopeless with his hands.

Afterwards, she sanded the plaster in Nick's room while she and Chris told each other their day: the old ritual. "Marina called when I was up on the ladder and I left plaster all over the house," was her sole adventure.

"What's up with Marina?"

"I can't even remember. She's like an eggbeater, isn't she? I don't know how she does her work."

"Her strength is as the strength of ten because her heart is pure. Who's she with now?"

"She's alone. Mike's in jail. She'll stay clear of him when he comes out."

"I don't understand a woman like Marina, bouncing like that from man to man."

"Her psychiatrist told her she wasn't monogamous."

"Jerry could have told her that."

"Well, he wasn't exactly, either. Do you know, we've known each other twenty years now?"

"I've always thought she was a strange friend for you."

"Ying and yang, I guess so — oh, I don't mean sex, Chris." Because he had flinched. "We complement each other."

"She hasn't your stillness, your peace. You're like a pillow. I rest on you."

She looked down and smiled at him, then. "I need her tur-
moil, I think. She lives my borrowed life. Sometimes she
makes me feel ashamed of my stodginess, but I love to hear
about the way she lives: she gets hurt, but she's so . . . alive."

"So are you."

"She says I should go back to painting."

"Do you want to?" He was flinching again.

So often in a marriage, she thought, you have to decide
whether to be good or to be honest.

"I don't think so," she said. "When I feel creative I work
on the house. People say it's a cop-out to give up your art. I
think, if you can give it up, it wasn't art."

Chris looked disapproving. "You were very good."

"Oh, precise; but I never took off. I hadn't the energy, I
think. Anyway, you and the kids need me, and I like to be
needed."

They went to bed early, after showering the flakes of plaster
out of their hair. In the morning a new job came in and Chris
was pleased and excited. He leapt off, leaving her a list of
things to do.

She didn't do them. She read the paper slowly, and sat
down to think about her life. Marina had lit some kind of fire.
What was she doing with herself but ageing slowly, in the service of other people, and was that right? What if Chris, who
was edgy these days, took off with someone less like a pillow?
What if the business failed utterly in some kind of depression?

Maybe I'll start drawing again, take a course somewhere,
try the Open Studio.

The fact was, she decided, that hers wasn't a marketable
talent. It had been a very small one, and without nurturing, it
would not have grown. What she liked to do with it now was
arrange anchovies perfectly on a salad.

Chris came home unexpectedly, found her moping. "What
are you doing, doing nothing?"

"Thinking."

"Where's the lens for the Nikon?"

"On the sideboard."

"Oh, yes; thanks."

He dashed out again. When he was happy his face filled out; his thinness did not show. Though he ate like a horse. She loved him the way she loved her house; they were both seemly and beautiful.

She sighed and made his phone calls. At least, in case something happened, she had a half-interest in the house. "Why am I thinking like that?" she wondered.

Later, Marina called again, as she had every day for years. Pat was impatient with her.

"Why are you snarky?"

"You know me too well."

"Well, give over, why?"

"Oh, I think about your life and about mine and I like my life but I don't like to feel square."

"Then find a lover. It would tone you up, do you good."

"Heavens, I wouldn't know how."

"Listen, is there something wrong between you and Chris?"

"There's something wrong between me and the world. I'm the last wife."

"Good for you. I couldn't stand it the twice I tried, but it's nothing against you. As long as you're doing what you want."

"Oh, I am; but I'm beginning to feel that I oughtn't to want what I want."

"Watch that number, Pat; it's a bummer. I've been everywhere. I ought to know."

A house, children, a garden; enough to do. Chris, who was sometimes her father, sometimes her friend, sometimes her youngest child. It was like the bland, perfect pictures she had drawn when she was out working, before she entered Chris's world. It frightened her: the whole world was upset and she was happy. She cut herself grating the carrots.

Marina called that night when they were in bed. Her sister had died. How could anybody die of a broken ankle? She was more irritable than heart-broken. Her sister had been limp, the brother-in-law was limp, none of the family could cope, she was the only one who had any money . . .

"I pray for that girl," Pat said as she hung up.

"You what?" Chris asked, suddenly awake.

"I pray for that girl."

"Do you still say prayers?"

"Not formal ones. But I do when I feel like it."

"I thought we agreed we didn't believe in God."

"Did we? I don't remember."

"Good heavens, woman. You're going back to the old, primitive things."

"It does no harm," she said defensively.

"I hate to see you falling back into superstition."

She lay back with her elbows behind her head and thought awhile. "Religion is private," she said. "I don't think you should tell me what to feel."

"You're bringing up my children. What have you taught them?"

"Nothing, except that if they feel like praying, it might help."

"Honestly, Pat. I thought you were a good rationalist."

She was half amused. He might be accusing her of having an affair. "Look, Chris, anything that can help you keep your still centre is good. You get drunk, sometimes, and spew out all your bad feelings. Do I object? Then why shouldn't I have little pleading conversations with the corner of the Lord I can't disbelieve in?"

He got up and paced around the bedroom. He ranted and raved. She had not realized that his rationalism was still so important to him. She was almost amused. She let him go on, and found herself saying she disagreed.

"Oh well," he said sulkily. "please yourself. Only don't go dragging the boys to church."

"Heavens, I couldn't."

"I'm astonished at you. All this time you've had a kind of secret life.'

"Haven't you? How can anyone know everything about another person?"

"I mean you expect Marina to go around casting hexagrams and chanting and taking up every new religion that comes along, but not you.''

Suddenly she felt him fall into sleep. She lay in the dark for a long time, warm beside him, and immensely more content. The reason her drawings had not been good was that they were too easy, too perfect; they did not reach out, or strive. Her life had a flaw in it now, and she felt better.

Madame Hortensia,
Equilibriste

Madame Hortensia, Equilibriste

I'm all right now, though I've had my uncomfortable patches. I have six children, and I hide behind them. They're very good about it. Every year I line them up in front of the picket fence and the privet hedge and take pictures of them, which we stick in the album. They're very good about it, except Amy. Not everyone is born with a happy nature.

Sometimes I get restless and think, I'll have to be moving on, but this year, I think, I'll be spared.

The only ones of the children who know about me are the oldest, the twins Yolande and Roland. They think it's fascinating; they want to get my old albums out, and read my life like a story, but I won't let them. It's bad luck to have ambition, I tell them. It's exercising overweening pride. It's taken me all these years to get humdrum. Don't spoil it.

"Yolande," I say, when I see her posing in front of the mirrors — she's pretty as one of Charlie's Angels and she knows it, but in a nice way — "don't get ideas about yourself. The only happy people here are the ones who are ordinary." She looks at me impishly, as if I'm an old woman who doesn't know any more which end is up, but she's sweet, she always says, "Okay, Mum," and buckles down to a little school work, not too much. I don't allow them to distinguish themselves unless they can't help it.

But I get uneasy. I don't want them to know about me. I don't want them to get spoiled. I want them to lead ordinary lives, as if they were the children of some ordinary woman. Mrs Wiggs of the Cabbage Patch, say.

We live on the outskirts of town, and it's a very small town. I don't see many people. I send the kids to the stores or phone to have what I need delivered. I call myself Mrs Robinson. I always liked Robinson Crusoe. The only indulgence I've allowed myself is their lovely garland of names, Yolande and Roland, Amy and Gwendolyn, Abel and Fortunatus (William Fortunatus, so he won't be beaten up at school).

Mr Robinson left some years ago, feeling somewhat overwhelmed by children and undermined by my fortune. It wouldn't have helped the children if I'd given my fortune away, so I kept it. We need it now. It's not as much as it seemed in the days when everyone was poor but me, and it wasn't my fault.

Goodness, I sound like Cardinal Newman, needing to apologize for myself. But the papers say we're in for another wave of over-achievers again and I can't bear the idea of people competing and rising above each other once more. All that battling and tattling. I'm old enough, just old enough, to see history repeating itself. Old enough too, that there won't be another Mr Robinson. (Once there were so many. I wonder now why.) So I might as well spend my evenings writing my story down. I wish the Cantcurl carbon wouldn't roll up in the rain.

Gwendolyn won the typewriter in a colouring contest. She's out at her ballet lesson. I didn't want her to take it but they're giving them free at the Public Library now. I said I wouldn't go to the recital.

Yolande and Roland are upstairs studying for their exams. Fortie's at band rehearsal, Abel's out delivering for the drug store, Amy's the only one at home tonight. Upstairs sulking.

Squeezing blackheads, likely. That's her style. She hasn't worn anything but black satin for two years. She's mourning her lost childhood, she says. They're a lovely, rowdy cheerful gang except for her. Nice normal kids.

I wish Yolande didn't want to go to Radcliffe.

I was born in St Thomas, Ontario, the town where Jumbo died, in 1930. My parents were on the verge of being elderly, and although my tiny little father kept a tiny little shop on Main Street next to the Kineto Theatre, we did not live in St Thomas. We only used the hospital. In fact, I have no idea whether the main street of St Thomas is called Main Street, and someone recently informed me that the theatre was called the Kineto for one month only; it was so called during the time when I was vouchsafed my only visit to The Glovery, where my father sold handkerchiefs, kid gloves and ladies' haberdashery — underwear — exquisite as himself. It was about six feet square, a miniature emporium crammed next to the theatre marquee, and he presided over it in a morning coat and grey moleskin spats, as dapper and tidy as his white moustache.

I don't know much about my parents. They eventually vanished as one's parents do, but without leaving much documentation behind them. I don't remember any cosiness with them, they were more like indulgent grandparents; they're like ''the little old lady and the little old man'' in a fairy tale when I think of them, not like the gritty slip-strap mothers and shirt-sleeve fathers of Canadian fiction.

They called me Mireille.

They were old when they had me. I suppose she — her name was Sylvia, which seems unmotherly to me — was forty-five when I was born, in 1930. And he was a good ten years older. And they lived out in the country, on the edge of a little village, quite apart from the community. He commuted to his store in a big purring Packard with a net in the roof, as grey, outside, as his spats.

They were lovely people, tiny and silver and delicate. Lovely, and it seemed to me, always in love with each other.

Everything they had was dainty and soft. Even if I was only their little half-chick, they called me, as I said, Mireille, and I grew up in their house like Tom Thumb in his little nutshell of a bed, covered and clothed with cobwebs. In those days there was no business of trying to bring up the abnormal as if they were like everyone else.

I was spoiled, and I was very happy. It was hard for me to learn to walk, but nurses and doctors didn't come into it. A man in St Thomas made me the most beautiful little contraption, half cane, half crutch, trimmed with bits of leather and silk so that it looked a little like a parasol. I hopped around the front lawn behind the cedar hedge, pushing it ahead of me. In no time at all I was mobile.

I don't think it was because of me that they lived quite apart from the community. I can't imagine them participating in the gross functions of an ordinary Canadian town, and the thought of Father putting his birthday pennies in the Rotary Box or marching in the 12th of July parade is grotesque.

They were from Toronto. Legend had it that they had met while working in office buildings across Adelaide Street from each other and had fallen in love like two toys in facing plate-glass windows. They had had, in their words, to scrimp and save in order to marry, but by the time I "came along" Father was doing well. Lacy handkerchiefs and fine underlinen were much in demand in St Thomas, even during the Depression.

All our visitors, except for Miss Mitcham, the Anglican minister's daughter who educated me, were from Toronto: stately men and women, hatted and gloved, soft voiced; though one of my mother's sisters, Aunt Zinnia, sometimes raised her voice and hooted with laughter when she said they'd meant to call my mother not Sylvia but Salvia.

Until I was sixteen, we were very happy.

Mother was what is known as frail. Her heart was as fragile as her floating chiffon afternoon dresses. Her wrists were too fine and thin to knit the heavy khaki socks required by the Red Cross for the war effort. She worked on complicated cob-webby layettes, and otherwise devoted herself to instructing Mrs Ruddy, the housekeeper, and a series of country girls, in

the delicate maintenance of the house. She took a great many
naps. Our only forays into the outside world took us to the
movies. She was fond of both Shirley Temple and Myrna
Loy. Esther Williams was a source of wonder to her. We went
at night, chauffered by Father. I think he spent the time playing poker, but I was not aware of the fact at the time.

I was not aware of many facts at the time.

When I was sixteen, my father was what they called
"stricken" by a heart attack. I went to his funeral in a wheelchair with a plaid car rug over my knees. A number of men in
black suits arrived at the house. Mother collapsed in tears.
Miss Mitcham turned her whole attention to her resuscitation
and my education came to an end. Soon the rest of the happy
dream faded, for my mother outlived my father by only six
months.

Curiously, I did not mind. I was involved in my own
dream.

Cosseted, sheltered, and protected, I was yet a child, and
not many children like to be sheltered. I had seen little of the
world beyond the hedge, for little of it filtered into our house.
We received one Toronto newspaper (which was extravagant
of us, as Father's executors pointed out), *Maclean's* magazine,
and *The New Yorker*. My mother's reading tended to be old
romances like *The Rosary* and *Captain Blood*, copies of which sat
in the glass-front bookcase in the parlour. She also liked
Browning and Elizabeth of *Elizabeth and Her German Garden*.
Miss Mitcham had taught me Ovid and Hesiod, a few poems
of Goethe and Schiller, and how to read enough French to
plough through *La Porte étroite* and *L'Education sentimentale*
(Miss Mitcham's taste was sophisticated for her time and
place). A little botany. A little Euclid. Mother's taste in
movies was unreal to say the least, though throughout the
war, news films supplied some sense that there was something
beyond our hedge. And the country girls invariably smuggled
magazines like *True Confessions* and *Photoplay* into the house, to
read on the toilet when they were supposed to be making the
beds.

The Public Library did not exist for my parents, but it did

for Miss Mitcham, who was kind enough to supply me with a certain number of her favourite authors. I read Scott and Stevenson, Jane Austen and George Eliot. Virginia Woolf and Edith Wharton. Of the Canadians, Grey Owl, Marjorie Pickthall, and Archibald Lampman. We discussed the matter of E. Pauline Johnson and decided she was not refined. I think Miss Mitcham shied away from anything too athletic. I had read Mother's copies of *Freckles* and *A Girl of the Limberlost* but not been impressed by them; they were from my world.

But I was, in my strange way, athletic. I could not spend my whole time doing lessons and reading. I had no talent for knitting and embroidery and the piano was out because I could not use the soft pedal comfortably and Mother had Headaches. Unless we were having company, which we seldom did, all the afternoons of my life were free, and I set about to use them.

Where does the child acquire this impulse to distinguish herself, set herself up above other people? Especially a child who has rarely met another child, knows no one of her own age?

We had a beautiful set of tea plates for use on special occasions. They were thin and white and gold banded and in the centre there were exquisite coloured engravings of acrobats: Mme Hortensia was the one I loved; Mme Hortensia in a scarlet corset, standing on one foot on the back of a horse; Mme Hortensia, *équilibriste*. For whose profession, it seemed to me, I was admirably suited.

During those years my father came and went like a lovely silver shadow.

Equilibriste. I had to be someone, distinguish myself somehow. I could not become a musician, that was clear, for I was not allowed piano lessons. I did water-colours with Miss Mitcham and made a mess of them. My handwriting was poor. How could I be a great beauty with a frizz of carroty hair which even Mrs Dodger, who came to the house each week to do Mother and me, couldn't make lie down without smelly pomades? I couldn't be Esther Williams. Myrna Loy.

"Capitalize on your assets, Mireille," Miss Mitcham was always saying. "You have linguistic ability; use it." But I had no desire to be a writer. Nothing, perhaps, to say.

In those days, everyone, to avoid tuberculosis, went down for a nap after lunch. We lived on the edge of the village, almost in the country. I was forbidden to go beyond the hedged front lawn, but behind the house there were outbuildings, old stables and barns, and an orchard. It was in the abandoned barn, in the orchard, and along the top of the wall that separated the orchard from the farm next door that I became Mademoiselle Mirella, Equilibriste. Nobody ever saw me, or at least nobody ever told. Perhaps we were a local mystery and there was no one to tell.

Mother's little half-chick, protected and cosseted, hopped outdoors for her exercise at naptime. Clearly, she was not dying of consumption. Mother's little half-chick went into the barn and shed her long, protective skirts. Mother's little half-chick, first on the saw-horse, then on the beam, then on the hanging rope another lot of children had used for a swing . . .

Mother's little half-chick tailored herself scarlet corsets from an old Chinese dressing-gown; saliva'd her eyebrows and rouged her cheeks; found in the attic a frilly parasol.

Birdcage in one hand, parasol in the other, exquisite in pink silk stockings she found in a trunk: really, Mireille!

No one ever saw and no one ever knew. And then they died.

Oh, I had read Dickens, too.

Being an orphan was not what it was cracked up to be. I went to live in Toronto in a very dull house in a very dull neighbourhood. My cousin Dick worked in a bank. He had everything sold and put into trust for me. There was a good deal of money. He called my father the Jew Bootlegger.

His sisters, my cousins Betty and Nancy, tittered when I went hop-hop-hop. Aunt Zinnia put all my fragile clothes in the washing machine and ruined them. She grumbled that I used her like a maid.

In the end, I had to take matters into my own hands. I had an allowance of five dollars a week and spent it taking a taxi to a theatrical impresario. Hop-hop-hop.

This is not a moral story. It simply is not done in this country — in most countries, in fact — to succeed in one's aims almost without trying. In addition, to live almost totally cut off from the world, then to tackle its most cynical side head-on and to survive almost without injury is very immoral indeed. It's as bad as turning ploughshares into swords. Why was I not broken on the rack? I suppose because I didn't know I was supposed to be. My parents had called me Mireille and I escaped from my thick-headed cousins (though not from my cousin Dick's investment advice) before they had a chance to teach me the techniques of defeat.

From the day I met Mr Zambala, everything was easy. He was extraordinarily kind and interested in my special abilities. He passed me along to his friend Mr Borodino, manager of a number of night club performers, because, as he said, for a person of my refinement it was important to avoid the carny shows.

Mr Borodino had a large, bouncing, happy family, and he took me home to live with them while we planned my career. The problem of my age was quickly solved with the discovery that my birth had never been registered; it was easy to lie about my age. Finances were a small problem, for my mother had given me her jewellery before her death, and it was good jewellery.

I had hated so-called ''family'' life at Aunt Zinnia's; with the Borodinos it was different. There were six children, all busy and buzzing with ideas. Chrissie was nearest my age. Unable to decide between being a seamstress and a nurse, she became my dresser and remained with me for ten years. We are still good friends.

I opened in Buffalo in October 1947, as Madame Hortensia, Equilibriste. I was supposed to be a French war widow. We thought it was better not to mention St Thomas because of Jumbo.

Buffalo led to better things — New York, then Hollywood.

In those pre-television days America was hungry for sensations, and America found them. I cut across the public imagination at just the right points and was written up in *Life* magazine.

Mr Borodino and I spent a lot of time working up material, for it was important to avoid the grotesque. Chrissie and I fabricated costumes that were delicate and discreet. It was important to maintain an image that embodied these characteristics.

In all, my performing life lasted, as I said, for ten years. I loved most of it, for I no longer felt cut off from what I have always called "the outside world," and I received a good deal of praise. In addition, for some reason I cannot fathom, men were crazy about me: I was sent flowers and candy and invitations after every performance and grew agile at hopping away from greasy Lotharios.

All good things come to an end, however, and by 1957, my popularity waning, Chrissie dying to leave me to live with her true love, I decided to marry.

This is where my lack of experience of the real world tripped me up: I was a poor picker.

The story of my life with George ought to be veiled in obscurity. It began well and ended very, very badly. He was handsome and spoiled and for a while he called me his Dresden doll. After Yolande and Roland arrived, he began to call me his freak. At heart a good little Victorian, I could not imagine that my marriage, like so many others contracted in the fifties and sixties, would end. I began to drink and soon found that the world was eager to shut its doors on a popular curiosity. The warbling little voice I had worked up for the stage sounded obscene when I bleated my banal tragedy into telephones. Friends disappeared in droves.

Fortunately, George, revivified by freedom, was too busy with a series of new girlfriends (a lion-tamer, a theatrical agent, a blind chanteuse) to claim the children. Just as I was collapsing in a sticky puddle of self-pity, Chrissie and my lawyer persuaded me to take Roland and Yolande home to

Canada and count my blessings.

I hated the idea at first, but with my savings and a stipend from George, I settled not in the modest sordidness of Aunt Zinnia's quarter, but on the edge of the Rosedale Ravine. I changed my name and took to making my forays on the outside world in a wheelchair, to avoid exhibiting my extraordinary talents. I was still attractive to men — odd how some of us have sex appeal and others don't and neither of us makes the choice — and met and married my Mr Robinson, producing with great rapidity Gwendolyn, Amy, Abel, and Fortunatus before he left for younger pastures.

When I look back on it all, I am amazed, but I also see what is wrong. Perhaps it was the Women's Liberation Movement that taught me this. To be different, to set oneself up above other people, even to chase the Borodino boys around the edge of a Buffalo billiard table, is to become an object, a freak. As my parents' little Mireille, I was a person; as Madame Hortensia, I was as unreal, as objectified, as one of the little figures on the Porcelain de Paris plates, as people on talk shows.

My children are splendidly normal, free of the birth defects Mr Robinson and George constitutionally feared. I live in the country now, at the edge of a small town with a good school system and plenty for the children to do. If you've seen one night club act, you've seen them all. I can no longer painlessly imagine myself hopping in disguised lingerie over the patrons' martini glasses. I do not know whence my desire to do so arose, but I wish it hadn't, for it caused me great and unnecessary pain. It is better to be plain Mrs Robinson with one's children in front of one like a privet hedge, a picket fence. I keep my acrobatics to myself, now, and Amy worries me with her black satin.

The Life of
Bernard Orge

The Life of
Bernard Orge

Did this story begin the year that I first saw Denzil playing hangman with the twins and the hanged man had my face? Or did it begin the year I was born? Or in the year of the Animals, when we all turned up at parties in furry vests and goatshair sweaters and shoes more suitable for hobbits than Torontonians? Or was it because the cultural grants were cut back that Bernard Orge and I got ideas about each other?

I had been thinking about change for some time, I suppose, because my boys, Victor and Hugo, had finally left home. I had been more or less through the mill with them — to put it more formally, they had accustomed me to change — but for their sake I had had for 18 years to maintain the personality of Mum for 12 or 14 hours a day, which was stabilizing. I felt, in fact, like a grindstone, the bottom one against which the gods grind whatever they do grind slow and fine; but there was something young in me too, that, watching them change out of their Upper Canada College uniforms into their splashed punk night uniforms made me think, I can do that. And then the news that they were leaving both me and Upper Canada (I didn't mind, Grandpa was paying) to form a punk rock band called Les Miserables shoved me one more step into the future and Bernard Orge.

I am a woman of a certain age and not a wildly attractive one if good bones are the major sign of beauty in women: mine have at most times been coated with a slathering of flesh that made my mother, who fed us on nothing but jersey cream, butter, and the yolks of double-yolked eggs, very proud. Even during my thin stages, I lacked distinction; but when I was twenty, the hallmarks of a marriageable woman were a big bust, long legs, and the ability to tolerate a girdle, so I didn't suffer.

For many years after Denzil succeeded in murdering, not me, but a strange woman passing down our street he mistook for me in his distraught state, I supported Victor and Hugo by being a kind of universal aunt to theatre companies and arts groups. The work was not highly paid, but the hours were irregular enough to accommodate childhood attacks of fever and measles and I-won't-go-to-school. I also attained a small reputation as a poet, and there were periods when, even unglamourous as I was, I swirled in the evenings around the streets of Toronto like a blown utilitarian leaf with people much younger and more attractive than I was. I enjoyed it, and it was important to me that the city was gradually becoming much more to me than the place where my grandmother had taken us out to the Diet Kitchen to have one lamb chop, one scoop of mashed potatoes, and one scoop of squash.

At first, the silence left by the departure of Victor and Hugo was so blissful that I barely missed them. Then I began to find myself a little distraught — this may have been about the time the authorities were thinking of letting Denzil out of Penetanguishene. I began to notice how visual taste had become. I began to think back to my childhood, when the superb thing in our life had been music and the opportunity to make music. And radio, that was the other thing. I thought of listening to the CBC Stage series on winter nights, Mother at the ironing board, doing whatever it was she did to Peter Pan collars, very

quietly, listening to the lines. Now that we were visual rather
than aural, things weren't as good for me, an ageing, boneless
poet: but the city was more satisfying, more liveable-with;
there was that.

So one night when I was managing the Polish mime troupe,
I went to Meyer's Delicatessen with them, and we all sat and
enjoyed its curious mixture of Vienna formality and New
York pizzazz. I tried to explain to them the great blasting
signs offering specials on pistachio cheesecake, and told them
what I knew of the framed show-biz personalities on the walls,
and I loved the way they responded with little cries and
gestures. I was very happy.

As I was standing at the cash register, I met Joe Crown,
whom I'd run into on and off for twenty years. "Hi," he said,
"never thought I'd see you in a place like this, you asshole
WASP female chauvinist poet." And he took off his Groucho
Marx glasses and put them on my nose.

Psychiatrists like you to change. Certainly when Hugo was
going through his bad patch, they roared at me, "You must
change, Mrs Elph." Joe put his Groucho glasses on my nose
and I looked into the mirror of Meyer's Delicatessen, past the
stylized grins of the Polish mimes, and I changed. I was Bernard Orge.

I turned my head in vanity towards my shoulder, preening
like a bird with my new beak. "Bernard Orge," I said.
"Thanks for the glasses, Joe. You may well have made one
person happy, watch out you don't get run over."

I walked out to take my troupe back to their hotel, and Bernard Orge was born.

Bernard Orge, I kept murmuring to myself. I am Bernard
Orge. Where does Bernard Orge live, I asked, fumbling for
the key of my inexpensive front door. I knew where Marge
Elph lived then, but not Bernard Orge. I knew nothing about
him, none of the essentials, where and how he lived, what race
his grandparents were. Was he Orge from Barley or Orge
from the Burial of Count Orgaz, from Orgasm, from *orgueil*,

pride? Or was there a word in Latvian or Finno-Ugric or Turkik, orge, that had a meaning all its own, like funk or putt?

Bernard Orge. I looked at him in the hall mirror. He was a distinguished fellow, short in the leg and the upper lips, perhaps; and his cheekbones weren't much. But what a nose! It might well be Jewish but it was just like the hook of my grandfather Will the Mill (as distinguished from his cousins Will the Hill and Will from over the Mountain) Macdonald. It sat very well on the face of Marge Elph. It was big enough to fill up the flat sea of her jolly face. It might not look better, I thought, if I had bifocal lenses put in the Marxian rims, but I would certainly see it better.

Meanwhile, I wondered, where did Bernard Orge live? What did Bernard Orge do?

I looked around me. The house was battered, serviceable, and even pretty. It was also an accomplishment, a roof I had managed to buy to shelter my babes from the wood. But it was as unromantic as Marge Elph.

This too will pass, I heard myself saying.

Well, I thought suddenly, why not? My secondary sexual characteristics are starting to disappear, and I was astonished when they appeared in the first place. I don't have lovers any more: the ones who used to like me were too downy and Victor and Hugo drove them from the paths of dalliance up the walls. Now my body is as ruined as any choir, I have big feet and I wear unisex Birkenstocks. There are as many men as women the same shape as me. My centre of gravity is shifting, and who notices me anyway now?

I went up to bed, leaving, as usual, the light on for Victor and Hugo. I flung myself on my bed. It wasn't my bed anymore. Surely Bernard Orge wouldn't tolerate this welter of quilts and hot water bottles and comforters and cats?

Next morning, I scanned the apartment ads, and the real estate pages as well. I wondered about selling the house. Even if Victor and Hugo come home now, I thought, their stay would surely be temporary; they'd stay a few weeks, complain about the food and one having a big room, one a little, and discover some good gig in another city and take off again; so why couldn't I sell the Ancestral Home.

My mother and father did that; the moment Father turned 65 he put the house on the market, bought a trailer, and moved to Florida. My sister and I were snobbish about the orange juice booth he and Mother ran, but I couldn't help noticing they were happy.

Denzil's parents hung onto the family home, which was one of those big, white, frame-and-shingle bastards that expect ten children every weekend. He was a judge, and she was afraid of him. The first time Denzil took me home, his mother set out the tea, and his father turned and said, "No applesauce, Etta? You're starving them." She put her face in her hands and burst into tears. I was appalled. Denzil's brother Maurice was 50, so it couldn't have been a new fight. Old Mrs Elph kept the house so the boys could come home, and of course they hated to. Maurice was good to his mother when they were dying in the same hospital, but I, who was somehow associated in her mind with Denzil's disgrace, stayed away until nearly the end, when she looked like a dormouse that had been swallowed by its teapot. I cried for her, and for all of us when she died.

No, I thought, Bernard Orge doesn't preserve only slightly ancestral homes for punk young men. I began to clean out cupboards, toss away ten years' jigsaw puzzles and games and hockey pads, and think hard.

I decided he lived in an expensive apartment on the waterfront and worked in the literary as opposed to the artistic department of an advertising agency. Unless he taught Old High German or medieval French.

I decided he hated chairs. They reminded him of the laps of old women in church, and he fears to see bloomer and garter. He had fashionable foam settees.

He had, I decided, a modern white kitchen with chrome

lighting and only one appliance: a kitchen machine that is a toaster as well.

He had, I decided, no Rodgers and Hammerstein and Hart records at all: only four Dennis Brain horn records and an album of Schubert lieder.

I set about getting rid of everything I could that had belonged to Marge Elph, middle-class and fustian and middle-aged. If Bernard Orge wouldn't have anything to do with it, I would chuck it.

In the course of those mad months, I had one wild stroke of luck. I ran into an old baby-sitter, a steady lad who had never disliked the twins, and discovered that he was studying the manufacture of prosthetic devices at George Brown College. Somewhat shyly, he set about manufacturing for me a nose to attach to my new black bifocal frames (the black toy ones were too weak to hold proper lenses). He insisted on the nose's being detachable, in case some hangover from my previous existence, like a passport, was to be put to use. His charges were very reasonable.

I don't recall that I have ever been so happy as during that period of my life, but there was one problem: I got so involved with Bernard Orge that I forgot to look for work. I had to rush out into the market and take the first thing I could get when the bank account was low, and that was a secretarial job where they simply couldn't stand my nose. I was fired within a week.

Within a fortnight, I had almost no money left. This amazed me. During the long haul of raising Victor and Hugo when I paid for everything but their school fees and uniforms, I had never been irresponsible about money. I had in fact become a compulsive bill-payer. Bernard Orge, it turned out, was quite irresponsible.

I investigated the real estate value of my house. The existing morgage was small enough to suit a clerk at Woolworth's and the taxes were not high, but I could not sell it for enough to buy Bernard a beautiful waterfront condominium. I decided that Bernard would have to drop his job in advertising, become a semi-indigent poet, and live where he might.

There was enough in my bonus savings account to cover a couple of months' mortgage and taxes, heat and light, and I considered myself fortunate. I decided to live on the food that inevitably piles up in one's kitchen cupboard, old boxes of cereal and cornstarch and pasta, tins of ancient anchovies and things that had once looked as if they might be good hors-d'oeuvres at parties that were never given. I used the money I found in all the coat pockets I could go through to buy a notebook in which to record the adventures of Bernard Orge.

It was a very amusing life. I got up in the morning and drank tea after I ran out of coffee, and herb tea after I ran out of India tea. When my subscription to the morning paper ran out, I started reading the encyclopaedia in the morning. I stopped smoking, felt better, though irritable for it, and wrote long, intense letters to Bernard Orge in my notebook. When that was full, I found odds and ends of paper in drawers and among the boys' school notes. I didn't go out much. There was nowhere to go. I decided that Bernard Orge was not a gossip, so I ceased to ring up my friends. Anyway, Julie was spending the winter in California and Nan had a lover in Newfoundland and was mostly away. Nobody called me.

I began, victory of victories, to get thin. I looked entirely elegant, I thought, with my great hooked nose. Perhaps Bernard Orge was a collector of incunabula.

In one respect, however, I made a basic miscalculation. I forgot to renew my prescription for heart medicine.

On the sixth of the twelfth month at six, as usual, I turned up at my specialist's office. "What have you done, Mrs Elph?" he asked in astonishment.

"I've lost weight and stopped smoking!" I said. It seemed odd to be called Mrs Elph, or indeed anything. Then I remembered he hadn't seen my nose before. So I said, "I got new glasses. I've never liked the old ones." I didn't explain that I was Bernard Orge, frail collector of early Rumanian icons.

"Have you been taking your Multihex?"

"I've been far too well, I'm afraid."

"Out of a job? Why don't you get Unemployment Insurance?"

"I've never done anything that offered it."

"You ought to have called me. There are ways of getting things."

"I've been perfectly happy. I feel wonderful. I more or less forgot, that's all."

"How can you say you're happy? Your heart's only half ticking, you've barely got a pulse. Now don't tell me you can't go back into The Unit because you've got twins. They must be forty by now."

"They're twenty and they have a band in Vancouver."

He made a phone call. "I want you at Admitting at two tomorrow afternoon. Go home now — here, take a taxi, for God's sake, and don't trip over anything as you go up the walk." He thrust a two-dollar bill at me. "Make arrangements for your cat and above all make sure you remember the name of your next of kin."

He was so savage I didn't tell him I'd got rid of the cats and my next of kin was Bernard Orge.

I rather liked the hospital. I was tired of pasta with awful sauces made from the spice rack and old Oxo cubes. One night we had lemon snow pudding for dessert and it seemed the whole justification of a past spent gagging down eggnogs. But I ate sparingly, not wanting to return to my original uncouth size, where there would be only coarse jobs for Bernard Orge and large trousers for me.

For a while, I tried to deceive myself that I had turned permanently into Bernard Orge, but while I lay in the hospital bed, my heavy spectacles on the table beside me, I realized that he and I were intertwined in a different way. He had become not a second self, but a sort of lover. I rather disliked the idea at first, because I had so wanted to change and was not managing to do so, but in moments of energy I began to write a few tentative little poems to him. They were better than the clumsy odes he tried to write about himself.

Medical students and interns came and pummelled me and

took case histories because my doctor taught at the medical school. Nurses rubbed my back, and it felt good to be touched after so long. I was fed and watered and I wrote and nobody said anything rude about my nose, though I heard some white-coats giggling in the doorway of the ward one day.

Finally, my doctor said I could go home the next day if I would first talk to a Dr Waterman, who, he claimed, was taking a social survey. I knew better, for Dr Waterman wore Dundreary whiskers and began to ask questions about my spectacles. I explained calmly enough that I disliked my real nose and saw no reason not to have a better one. "Do you have a different name when you wear them?" he asked.

"No," I lied. There are hawks' wards and handsaws' wards and it wasn't for this I'd kept up my medical insurance.

"Isn't it hard to get jobs wearing them?"

"It's hard to get jobs."

"Have you tried, recently?"

"I've been resting, as we say in the theatre. I'll try when I feel better."

He looked at me fiercely. "You ought to figure out what you've done all your life!"

"I've done Denzil and Victor and Hugo and a book of poems and been a freelance universal aunt!" I said loudly, surprised at my own vigour. "I got sick of picking up after people. I'll figure out something to do."

"When?"

"When I finish the cornstarch and the lentils."

"A woman your age shouldn't be too proud to type."

I forebore to tell him about my typing and Bernard Orge's.

"Get up every morning in good time!" he said. "Eat a balanced diet. Exercise! Think healthy thoughts. Occupy your mind. You are indulging in the worst sort of idle decline. You're not sick enough for a disability pension, you're too young for a nursing home. Here, take a taxi home." He held out a two-dollar bill.

I took it, packed up my notebooks and underwear and pills and left. Doctors know a lot, but they still think taxis are two dollars. I was shaky but smug when I opened the door. On the mat with my mail was a free sachet of instant coffee. It looked delicious.

I drank it and read my letters. Victor and Hugo were alive, well, and so far unarrested in Vancouver. They wondered if they could borrow ten thousand dollars to buy a stake in an oyster farm. The hydro bill could be handled. My hospital insurance was due again. And a woman I knew called Anne Salting wondered if I would take care of a series of chamber music concerts for her, and hearing I had been ill, enclosed a hundred dollars on account.

I sat at the dining-room table and re-read the letter. It was over, this episode of irresponsibility and starvation. Things were beginning to happen again. In my anxious joy I took off my glasses and twisted them and broke off Bernard's nose.

It lay, pastel and out of focus, on the ground by my feet until I put my spectacles on again. I stared at it, and got up and looked in the mirror over the mantelpiece. I saw a rather sweet-looking, frail, old woman with a vapid face, a little nose like a child's, and blue eyes much magnified.

I hunted for a decent scrap or two of paper and wrote letters. One, thanking Anne for the cheque and saying of course. She was my way away from Dr Waterman and the handsaw ward.

A second, directed to the ''Companions Wanted'' column of *The Globe and Mail*, advertised for a new friend for Bernard Orge. I felt I owed him that.

Ten days or so later I had organized myself a rather smart and boyish image with a new short haircut (white hair is a different texture from one's old mouse brown and cuts better) and the only clothes I could find to fit, which came out of Victor and Hugo's dresser drawers. I came in rather tired from a meeting with Anne, took a pill, and fixed myself a cup of tea. The doorbell rang, and I hardly knew what to make of it. The gas meter had been read the day before.

There was a tall, rather melancholy-looking man on the doorstep. ''My name is Bernard Orge,'' he said. ''I understand you have some letters for me.''

"Four, so far," I said. "Won't you have a cup of tea?"

"Gratefully," he replied. There was a faint hint of an accent. Central Europe educated in England, perhaps. I took his coat and ushered him through to the dining-room. He looked around. "I rather fancied modern furniture for a time. There was to me a basic obscenity about the laps of chairs. But because of a back ailment I have had to conquer that feeling. You wouldn't be thinking, perhaps, of renting a room?"

Through his thick glasses he gave me a long and penetrating stare.

"What do you do?" I asked.

"For the moment, I am situated in a minor position in an advertising agency. In Europe, I was a well-known poet and iconographer. I also," he said, "have a cat."

I thought for a moment. He could be the Boston strangler; he was more likely to be a domestic nuisance, the demanding Ruritanian equivalent of Victor and Hugo. He was only vaguely handsome, and marginally clean, and he was certainly older than me.

"Can you cook?" I asked.

He smiled broadly, and showed me a pocket certificate from the Ecole Gastronomique in a small town in France. Out of my cupboard I brought the bottle of stimulating spirit which was the last of my purchases from Anne's hundred dollars. "To your very good health," he said.

I don't know what he did about the letters. My friends say we're an unlikely couple, myself so serious and Bernard full of rather ghastly dated jokes. He doesn't work much. He says he suffers from European spleen. Oddly enough, he likes New Wave rock, but he's good about turning the radio off when I come home. I expect some day I'll come home and find he's simply vanished.

There's still a tiny piece of plastic nose stuck to my glasses. It rubs and makes a red spot on my nose some times. Bernard asked me what it was one day, but I didn't tell him.

The Country Doctor

The Country Doctor

She had known she was going to enjoy this trip. There was no reason not to. She had had a busy winter and her ordinary life had seemed extraordinarily difficult, her voice rising every day to a higher pitch as she chivvied her son Simon through his duties, argued with editors, hurried through her work. Perhaps, she thought later, they had sent her away on purpose. Never mind, she was delighted to be here. Never in her life had she made so little fuss about finding a housekeeper for Simon, blocking out a series of interviews, dealing with photographers.

And indeed here everything had gone astonishingly well. She had liked the people she was made to see: they took her in like a long-lost friend. The town made her catch her breath. There was nothing else like it in Canada; early in the morning the sun sparkled on the granite wharves with a magical charm and innocence. She, who was most pleased when her eyes were pleased, revelled in it. The cynicism she had had to learn to protect herself from her imagination fell away: she walked naked of fear, light-headed, up the hill from the hotel to the party Tom Parsons was giving for her going away.

It was a funny party, and it got funnier as the evening grew old. They had started with mugs of tea flavoured with something Tom's father made in the back country; they went on to punch made of something Tom's wife Maureen's mother made in another part of the back country. It should have been nauseating but there was an astringency to it that also created a great thirst.

Most of the guests at the party were men. This was not, Maureen explained, a great place for baby-sitters. She sat by Diana, and once, when a joke was too broad for her taste, said, "Ah now, cut that out, Pete; Diana's here to write us up for her magazine and she'll think we're all bells and blisters." Diana had an impression that the expression was an edited version of something else. She started to giggle and had a hard time stopping. The others seethed into laughter with her. Then Maureen moved them all into the kitchen where there was a great round table loaded with pies and cakes. She made plain tea this time.

"Oh," gasped Diana, "I haven't had such a good time in ages."

"Don't they treat you well in the city then?" one of the men asked.

"It's been such a foul winter that people who don't even believe in astrology say our stars are crossed: blizzards, strikes, floods, breakdowns: you know."

He nodded wisely. "Most of us are damned glad to be out of the rat race."

"So you should be," she said, catching onto the lingo a bit. There was a pause.

"You aren't married, then?" another one asked.

"Not any more."

"It's bad on your own, then?"

She avoided her questioner's eyes and stirred her tea rapidly. "Not so bad: you get your own way a bit more. But it's been an awful year."

"Oh, we have them here too," Maureen said briskly.

"Give her another cup of tea, Tom. Now, tell us more about the great world. Do you think they'll switch over to the Tories there?"

Someone muttered about the fickleness of Hogtown. Diana shrugged. It wasn't the right time of night to talk politics, and the concerns of her Toronto friends were relatively meaningless here. "Oh well," she said as lightly as she could. "There are the ins and the outs, aren't there? And when things go bad you get the feeling you'd be better with the outs."

Tom clapped his hands loudly in her ear. "Well done," he shouted. "Ross, you should have known better than to ask her about politics but you can see she's been trained in a good school." The way he said it made her feel like a child or a toy.

Ross began to cough and sputter, and a man named Kevin thumped him on the back. "Never takes a day off, that one," someone said. She looked up at Kevin. He had a long face and a long nose that cast a shadow on his upper lip, and flaming red hair. As he thumped at Ross he looked her straight in the eye.

Maureen was a big, good-looking woman. It must have been two in the morning but she looked as fresh as she had when she opened the door. Now she thrust the teapot over towards Ross and Kevin. Kevin stopped his thumping, produced a silver flask from his inside pocket, and handed it to Diana. "Put some of that in your tea to take the acid off."

"Now Kevin, she'll go home making remarks about boozing among the friendly natives," said Maureen.

Diana took a little, just a little, smelling it as she capped the flask and handed it back. It was Scotch.

Everyone watched her as she sipped from her cup.

"Now don't give her any more or she'll miss her plane," said Maureen, bustling among the cups.

Diana knew she should say she was going; the silence had set in that meant the party was over. But she was glassy-eyed, somehow rooted to her chair. She sighed, put her head on one hand and said rather thickly, "You're all marvellous and I'm glad you've been good to me.''

"I'm not only marvellous, I'm practical," said the red-headed man. "I'm going to take you home."

There was a strange kind of silence again. Diana looked at Maureen. "I'd be glad of the ride," she said, and winked, "if he's safe."

Maureen put her head to one side like a bird. Kevin stared at Maureen. Diana pretended not to see either of them. Kevin said slowly, "I'm safe as houses, dear."

One of the men, who was obviously drunk, put his head on the table and started to giggle. "Well then," Diana said as briskly as she could, "let's be off." She said her good-nights and promised to phone Tom and Maureen before her plane left. She walked down the wooden sidewalk leaning a bit on the red-headed man. "No offence meant," she said.

"No offence taken."

He put her into the car like an old-fashioned gentleman. As he fumbled for the ignition in the dark he said, "I like people to put their seat belts on." Then he leaned over, breathing an enormous waft of whisky at her, and pulled hers over her like a long, flat snake. As they drove down the hill, he said, "So you think you've seen everything here in a week?"

"Of course not. They allow me a week, that's all. And I have to get back to my boy."

"Is he a good boy, then?" The car purred like velvet under his voice. It was a heavy voice, but a courteous, educated one.

"No more than most boys. Sometimes. I don't know . . ."

"They're not easy to bring up alone."

"You can say that again."

"Are you getting the eight o'clock plane, then?"

"No, they said that one would be fogged, probably. I don't go till five."

"That's the better choice. If you've got a moment, perhaps you'd come and see my place then."

She was only half surprised. "No," she said firmly. "I'm far too tired."

"What I meant, Miss Diana, was my house: it's considered a show-place. And furthermore, it's right here."

"You may have to hold me up."

"I've done that to people before. I won't keep you long. Tom's a fine fellow but I don't approve of their country hooch; you never know what's in it." They went up two steps from the sidewalk and along another walk. She could tell they were near the harbour from the salt in the air. They went up shallow steps to a hollow wooden verandah. She made out a wide front door with coloured glass etched with flowers on either side of it. He fished an old skeleton key out of his pocket and opened the door. "I should know, I'm their doctor," and pointed to a brass plate beside it. "Kevin Morrison, M.D."

The light in Maureen's kitchen had been dim. She realized she hadn't had a good look at him. The light here was no better. She sensed him beside her, big, stiff, giving off heat and whisky. "I don't usually meet doctors socially," she said, "or else they say they're something else."

"You can't hide what you are here."

He moved cumbrously in front of her and stabbed at a mother-of-pearl light button. "Here we are."

She was at the foot of a wide mahogany staircase with curving bannisters and broad steps. On the landing there was a suit of armour and then the stairs branched into two directions. It was a very grand house indeed. "Oh," she breathed like a little girl.

"I wanted you to see it before you go. They call it Kevin's castle."

"It's beautiful. You live here all alone?"

"Since my wife has been gone. There's a woman comes to do for me. They tease me a bit about it but I don't mind. My mother and her mother put everything they had into it, and I don't want it changed." There was a taste of authority in his voice. It came from doctoring, she supposed. He took her by the hand and she let him. Lately, she thought, I've been running into men who don't know what they want.

He opened a door on the right and took her into a room: it was a Victorian parlour with tables with knobs, a marble fireplace, and two twisted love-seats, the back-to-back kind you see mostly in cartoons. Great swags of velvet at the windows. "Do you use it?"

"You're a practical woman. I like you. No." He led her through more doors into a dining-room with crystal vinaigrettes on a big carved sideboard. "No, I mostly use my consulting rooms on the other side."

From the dining-room they went into a pantry, then a vast kitchen where the only new things were a refrigerator and a glass vase of coffee simmering on an iron stove. He turned the stove off somehow, and reached into a cupboard. "Milk and sugar?"

"Black."

"Hard on the liver. And the tongue. Come on, I'll give you the rest of the grand tour and we'll come back."

The staircase creaked. He took her, as usual, to the right. "They were shipbuilders in the old days," he said. "They cared about carpentry. I don't know where they got the tin suit. She used to travel."

"Is she dead?"

"Oh, long gone. She wasn't much of a pleasure. People with taste are not, on the whole. But she cared."

She followed him up the staircase, dead with drink and fatigue, thinking, I've met so many men since I left Jack, and in another country there'd be portraits on these walls: that's what's funny, no portraits. "There are no portraits," she said, for something to say.

"That wasn't our style. I suppose there wasn't enough for pictures, or she got rid of them. There might be some in the box-room, if you'd care to look."

It's when I'm tired I'm whiny, she thought. She wanted to whine now. She said nothing, just followed him. "This was her spare room," he said, "if I recall," to a roomful of heavy furniture, quickly lighted and turned out. "And, this was Mama's." A grand, large, airy room complete to the pink flowered jug and basin on the wash stand, with a handsome canopied bed.

"Did your wife live here?"

"No, she wouldn't stay. It drove us apart. What would you think of it?"

"I'm not the domestic type," she muttered weakly.

"I thought not." He laughed, and took her hand firmly. "Oh," pulling some drapes aside at the galleried end of the stairs, "nobody is, these days. Can you see out there?"

Out over the harbour the dawn was coming up, rosy-fingered indeed. He moved towards her, closing the curtains again as he did so, and slid an arm around her. He was much taller than she was and she felt small and for a moment, just a moment, safe. Then she looked up at him and his very big, very white face and saw that it was crinkled and cracked with a thousand wrinkles, as if he had suddenly aged or cracked like the glaze on a jug; his mouth was a wide, red gash, and she was afraid of him. She thought, his hair's not natural, it's too red and too neat, like a piano-tuner's wig. I have to stop picking up men, there could be bodies in those big wardrobes. But it was too late to turn away and she let him kiss her. His skin was dry and harsh, but his mouth was soft and not too probing.

He resumed the tour as if nothing had happened. "There are a lot of little rooms over the kitchen," he said, "little bedrooms and box-rooms. And here's the one I like best."

It was a big cheerful room with a fireplace with carved marble faces and two velvet armchairs before it. She sank down in one and rubbed her cheek against its shoulder. "I'm tired, Kevin," she said, "too tired to think or to feel or to take in any more. I want to go home like a bad song."

"Give me your hand."

She was hesitant, but she knew her hands didn't come off like rubber gloves so she held one out. He pulled her to her feet with it and half led, half carried her, to the bed. She was going to protest, but her head touched the pillow and she fell asleep.

In the morning she woke, thinking, where am I, what have I done, my head, the red-headed man . . . She remembered words but no touch. She looked over to the other side of the bed; sure enough, it was untouched. She felt herself. She had all her clothes on but her jacket and her boots: a gentleman. A man of honour. On the night table beside her there was a piece of paper, a glass of water, two aspirins. "Back at ten," the piece of paper said. It was from a prescription pad.

She got up, full of guilt. I'm like him, I'll never get used to the new ways, she thought. Waking up in a strange bed, put there by a strange man; it's too much for me. Her mouth tasted like old, rotten clay and her head banged its brains against its bone. Hooch, she thought. Screech. Ouch. She gagged the water down. Then heaved herself out of bed and looked out the window. Sun glinted on the harbour. But not very high. It was only seven by her watch once her eyes came in focus. Well, she thought, at least he isn't here with me. I could have sworn he would be. An odd man: an odd house. Under the lamp, he looked like a puffball: touch him and he'd fly away.

No matter who or what or without whom she'd been with she felt dirty, soiled: a week rushing around intruding on people's lives, a week pretending she wasn't there, barging in, leading them on, remembering. A week without being herself. And now, instead of a motel bed, a brass bed with an embossed cotton spread and a note beside it. She tried to think what to do and decided the worst thing here was to go back to the motel too early: everyone is visible in the dawn. She went into the bathroom next door and turned on the taps on the sphinx of a tub. They gushed brown, then they cleared. They were no worse than her, she decided, as she got in. The towels were white, and the wash-cloths, and the bathmat.

She got out, refreshed and instead of her clothes (back at ten, puffball or wig or not) she put on a pleated white cotton night-shirt that hung on the back of the panelled white enamelled door. Took her own clothes into the bedroom, draped them as modestly as possible on the near velvet chair and crawled back into bed. Slept. Again. Good. So often she could not.

Woke again. Brilliant sun pouring in but something between . . . what? A large face, white: big-featured. I remember the mouth, she thought. She lay like a baby, blinking, staring up. He bent towards her. A telephone rang. He left.

What a big face, she thought, broad in the cheeks, wide-mouthed. Something about the eyes, I don't know what. Red hair, still. Not so much a kind face as a blank one. The crinkles are gone. Must be a . . .

Her morning body was stirring now. She missed him. A little. She had only known him a little.

He came back. She was lying there, patient. She had remembered he was a doctor. "There's been an accident in the woods," he said. "I can't even take you to the motel. The ambulance is picking me up." He ran a finger along her lips. "I'm sorry."

"It's okay," she said, because, what else? She didn't know him. "Take care of them, huh?"

"I will. If you want a taxi, call the Vets."

"Okay, off you go." As if to Simon, or so many other men.

He was gone. She got out of bed and dressed and tried to make the bed as exquisitely as the other side of it indicated. She failed, but her effort was respectable. Then she turned and went to hang up the night-shirt. She was finishing her period and had left a spot. She looked around at the exquisite room and quickly, furtively, scrunched the night-shirt into a ball and put it in the bottom of her purse.

On the way downstairs, she looked at the house again. She saw it this time as a stage, a proscenium arch. The hall was grander than the rooms around it: they had started big and finished small. Of course there were no pictures.

Then she remembered that some time in the middle of the night she had seen herself as the mistress of this house, failing to dust its grand bannisters. Keeping Simon from scratching things. Stoking the stove, ordering the retainer in the mob-cap about. It would be easier, she thought, to live without imagination.

She made sure the door was on the latch behind her and made her way down the bumpy street to the motel. Flounced onto her bed, read her notes again, organized her packing, made up her face again. Ran the powder over it with the odd feeling that it, too, would fly away. Remembered the red-haired man's face under the landing light, fractured by a fractured lampshade, vulnerable, powdered as a dusty miller's, old. Then his face in the morning, hanging over hers. Simon's, she thought.

Maureen called at noon. They had lunch in the coffee shop and there was time to put in till the evening plane. "Kevin took you home all right?"

"Sure, fine."

"He's a card, that Kevin."

"Is he?" Rather I should probe, she thought, than let Maureen.

"Oh, I was so mad at him letting on he was a bachelor and him with his wife and five kids and that museum of his where his office is."

"Museum?"

"His mother's house. The Pigott Museum. After her mother. It runs in the female line with them: the money, not the red hair. It's where his office is. Didn't he take you there? We all thought he would."

"I'm afraid I got out of the car and went right to sleep."

"Oh, he does that whenever he can pick up a woman, takes them back there and shows off the house and talks about his mother."

"Perhaps I ought to go up to the museum, then," she tried to fend Maureen off, "and put it in my article?"

"Oh, I wouldn't bother. It's just an old house, now. My daughter Eileen works there on the weekends. It's through her I know he takes women there. Poor Annie has her work cut out for her, looking after kids for the grand Dr Morrison. He's a real pig, I tell you, a pig."

"Honestly, Maureen, he left me off and I was too tired to notice. If he was Casanova himself, I would still have fallen dead asleep.'' Though inside herself something was merrily telling her stories about night-shirts.

''You've had a good time here, then?''

''I really have, and I'm grateful, Maureen.'' Her body stirring for something quite other. ''And you and Tom made it possible.'' Not hypocritically: they did.

If she was very hung over, so was Maureen. They held their hands out on the table but lacked the co-ordination to make them meet. In the end, she went back to the counter and asked to extend her stay another day. The girl said, ''If you're getting the five plane, no one else is coming, I can let you get away with it.''

''Will you wake me up?''

''Sure. If you can sleep, love, you probably need it.''

But she could not sleep; her nerves were stretched and her temples still pounded with the hangover. She lay rigid as a bow on the bed and at last sprang up. ''I'll at least find out the truth,'' she thought. She looked in the telephone directory and plunged out her door.

The motel was on the harbour; the museum was on the top street along the side of the hill that limited the growth of the town. The home address of Kevin Morrison was on a street parallel to both, a narrow street that looked as if it ought to be cobbled, so narrow the telephone lines were attached to the stone houses themselves, not on poles. The front doors of the houses were level with the sidewalk. In case they opened outwards she walked in the road.

Number seventeen had a bow-window, with a couple of panes of bottle glass. In the window was a small, red-headed child and when she went past it pressed its belly against the window, squinted and stuck out its tongue malevolently. She turned and almost ran back to the motel.

''Oh, it's you,'' said the girl at the desk. ''The five plane's been cancelled and Dr Morrison will be around to pick you up for tea at half-four.''

So that was that.

He looked more reliable in the last of the daylight. As if, this time, his long face would not threaten to slide off. "Hair of the dog," he said, "I think. We'll just go on up to the house."

Oh God, she thought, what story's he going to string me now. She began to demur.

"Nonsense," he said firmly. "You can't eat in that coffee shop again, old Mary's never heard of anything but frying in whale oil. And if you want to drink you'll have to go into the men's and it's no place for a lady." So they lurched up in his car.

This time he took her into his consulting rooms, which were large and shabby. There were two leather chairs and two great black rockers that were covered with something between imitation leather and horsehair. She remembered the stuff from her grandmother's house. It stuck to children's bare legs like adhesive tape. She sat down on one of the leather ones. He disappeared into what looked like an examining room and returned with whisky and glasses and ice. "Now," he said, "to the inevitable."

She thought of the red-headed child, the house on White-side Street. "What I can't make out," she said, "is, are you married or are you not?"

"I'm as married as you. Look, there's something you didn't see last night I want to show you. Don't be afraid, I'm not Lothario. Come up the grand stairs again."

They got to the top and went round to the front under the hanging light. "Oh," he said, "but first . . ." and put his arms around her. She looked up at him, curious to see if his face would again begin to disintegrate. She looked right into his eyes and saw nothing there but narrow pupils, a frighten-ing intensity. She closed her eyes. She heard a harsh little birdlike voice saying "You're just another one, just another one. One of the many, many, many. And he always begins here, right here. He's a bad, bad man and of that there's no doubt."

"What's wrong?" he whispered.

She shivered. "Cold, I guess."

"Never mind, I'll warm you. We'll go down now."

Downstairs in the leather-chaired room she said, "Look, I don't know anything about you. Maureen says you've a family, you say you're on your own. . . .I don't like fouling another woman's nest."

The telephone rang. He picked it up at once, looking away from her. Scribbled something on a pad. Sighed and stood up.

"I didn't think you were the sort to fuss," he said. "I'm as free as you are, that's the truth of it. But not quite free enough. I've got to go, Mrs Heaps has taken a turn, but it's not far. I won't be long. You can stay or go as you like. If you stay there's a ham in the pantry there to have a bit of. If you go . . . well, remember, I like you."

He hitched up his trousers, straightened his tie, picked up his bag and went out.

She decided to finish her drink and thought, at least I'll sleep tonight. She found an old *National Geographic* in the piles of magazines on the table and began to leaf through it and dozed off.

When she woke with a start, it was dark, and there was a creaking noise. She reached up as if she knew it was there and pulled the cord of an old-fashioned standard lamp. One of the black rocking chairs was creaking. She wondered if he'd come and gone and left it rocking but when she got up to see it, there was neither dent nor warmth to the seat.

Outside, the wind had risen. She remembered the house was high on the hill. Somewhere a branch was groaning against a wall. Somewhere a shutter was flapping. Gingerly she stepped out into the great hall and listened. It was one of the front shutters, surely. He'd be pleased to find her there when he came back. She'd just fix the shutter and come down and have some of that ham.

At the top of the stairs she switched on the great lamp and stood and listened. There was no sound of the banging shutter now. Instead, as she moved under the lamp, the voice she had heard earlier, a bird-screeching malevolent voice, said, "He's gone, I told you, he always goes, he's better drowned, isn't he?" and began to cackle and laugh.

You don't have to be gullible to panic at a voice like that, she said to herself as she fled down the stairs. You don't have to believe in things that go bump in the night to be scared of them. She lit into the consulting room, scribbled on the pad by the phone "You are late, call me at motel, D.," grabbed her purse and skittered over the verandah to the street. Ham or no ham, she thought, I'm going to bed. Which she did.

Early, early in the morning the telephone shrieked at her. She answered groggily, hardly knowing where she was. "Kevin's gone," Maureen said. "Is he with you?"

"No," she said.

"I'm not collecting evidence, I have to know where he is."

"Not here. I haven't seen him since last night."

"What time last night?"

"About six."

"I'll be right over."

Oh God, she thought as she threw on her clothes, I get in these messes, why did I get involved? how the hell? . . . And Maureen was pounding at her door.

"You'll think me an idiot or a detective," she panted, "but I'm that scared. Old Mr O'Connor was taken bad last night and they couldn't find him anywhere and it's the fifteenth of May and I've such a . . . Tell me what happened."

So she told how she had gone up to the house with him. "I wanted to get the story straight. You said he had a wife."

"Oh he did indeed once. And such a wife!"

"Is she gone?"

"She was a jealous little bitch, that one, and no better than she should be. Now tell me, you said he got a call . . .?"

"About half past six, perhaps earlier. He said he wouldn't be long. A Mrs Heaps."

Maureen turned white. "A Mrs Heaps! What happened then?"

"I fell asleep. When I woke up it was dark. One of the rocking chairs was swaying and a shutter was banging. It was too spooky. I got out."

"You didn't go upstairs, then?"

"As a matter of fact I did . . . to try to find and latch the shutter."

"There's no shutters on that house, though there were on the other. Now, tell me Diana, this is serious, see, nothing to do with you — you're both lonely why shouldn't you . . ."

"Annie and the children?"

"Annie's his sister, and keeps the house on Whiteside Street. She has two of her own as well. I think one's Tom's, the rapscallion, but that's neither here nor there. What did you hear, then, upstairs?" Maureen was leaning on the dresser, clenching her fists until her knuckles were white.

"Hear? hear? Well, the shutter stopped." Diana closed her eyes, then remembered. "Maureen, I could swear I heard a voice saying 'He always does it here. You're one of many. He's better drowned.' "

"My God," said Maureen, and began to dial again. "Tom, Tom, drag the pond," she said. Slammed the receiver down. Then she put her face in her hands and started to cry.

"I wish you'd tell me what all this is about," Diana said quietly.

"Oh, if I did, you'd only put it in your article."

"I certainly wouldn't. I've made a fool of myself."

"Look, I'm going out there now. I just hope you aren't right."

"Wouldn't Mrs Heaps . . .?"

"That was her name before she got her hands on him, the bitch. You get some breakfast now and I'll come back and tell you what's happened." Maureen stood up, taller now, and somehow older. They're all related, Diana thought.

Diana shook her head as if to get water out of her ears and went to the coffee shop. She felt as if everyone was staring at her. She waded through her ham and eggs as stolidly as she could. I must be crazy, she thought, or they must be. Announcements do not come from puffball lamps. Reality exists. Reality must exist. If it doesn't exist here it does at home and I hope I can get there soon.

She was on her second cup of weak coffee when Tom slid

into the booth across from her. "He's gone," he said in a quiet voice.

"I don't understand."

"You wouldn't. It's a long old story. There's no Mrs Heaps. That was her name when she lived there, out by the pond."

"He said it wasn't far, he wouldn't be long."

"He was a broken man."

"I didn't help him. I thought he might just be fooling around."

"She said it was him or her. In the end, it was both of them. They ate each other up, as if it was the poem, like."

"It's really beyond me."

"It's beyond all of us. Some things are. There's a plane laid on at ten."

"Was he in the pond?"

"Oh, in the pond all right."

"And his face?"

He gave her a long look, as if he was going to be sick. "You saw that too. You saw that too. And you never knew you were one of us before, did you?"

She turned away and began to cry.

In the hour before the bus was to leave for the airport she clambered up the hill and let herself into the museum of the house. Inside the door she grabbed an old blackthorn stick from a Chinese umbrella stand. She ran up the stairs, banging against the armour on the landing, not stopping to see what happened behind her. She ran along the top corridor to the front, to the great hanging lamp; she hit it a shattering blow. Glass flew around her and a cloud of old dust and dead moths flew out. The front hall was still afloat with moths and shards of glass as she banged the door behind her.

In the plane, she sucked her knuckles and whimpered for him.

A month later she was having dinner with Oliver Crown. "You've been there," he said, naming the town. "What's it like?"

"Oh, picturesque," she said evasively.

"I know that, love, I read your article. But there must be more to it than that."

"I don't know, Oliver, there's just people, like anywhere else."

"I've been asked to go there. Some rigamarole about a ghost in a pond."

"The Spook of Randal's Cove? Honestly, Oliver! You don't believe in stuff like that. You'd do much better," she said, modestly muddling in her fruit salad, "to stay here and marry me. Simon needs a father."

He looked at her long and hard. "Are you being straight?"

"Sort of," she said, playing with her fork, staring at the scar on her hand.

"It sounds," he said quietly, "like a good idea."

She sighed with relief.

There From Here

There From Here

No one else knows what it's like, she thought. No one else knows what it's like. She was bitter.

She was sitting bolt upright. He sprawled, but his tie was tied right. Something she couldn't have taught him at home.

There they were, climbing up the escarpment. She remembered it from her tenth birthday, racing around the Monument, falling. There was still a scar on her knee. In spring, and early fall, the roads were heavenly around here, there were waterfalls dripping with hepatica and maidenhair fern and shimmering yellow and orange stands of birch and maple. The limo climbed steadily, like a flat-bottomed turtle. It was an awful day: everything grey, between autumn and snowfall. The world was made of frozen mud and dried corn-stalks, not a good thing to see.

She spent the morning going through her phone book thinking, could he? could she?

The one thing she had failed to learn to do was drive a car. And the school was out in the middle of nowhere. For obvious reasons. How many people had she used to cart him there? No one was available this Thursday: Alice was at the hospital with her mother, Phil was teaching, Joe was doing his bar exams. Finally, she had called a man who used to be a writer and now owned limousines. He gave her a price: eighty dollars. On top of the school fees, eighty dollars. It wasn't right.

The boy, her boy, lay sprawled like a broken doll on the seat before her. All yesterday they'd been in court. The judge had reserved decision until today. The lawyer phoned at two and said, "He's going back. Right away. It's a court order."

The man who drove the limo was a friend of the writer. His name was Walter. He was an old man and did this sometimes to add to his pension from the army. He knew about boys.

On top of the escarpment there were two places she'd always wanted to visit. An antique dealer's and a nursery that sold old roses. In the embarrassment of asking other people to drive her and the boy, she hadn't managed to ask them to let her visit either. It was a total embarrassment, this whole thing. How had she managed everything so badly? Though the school was doing him a world of good.

He had spent his first two months running laps and writing suicide notes to his father, who sued for custody. She had had to sit in court listening to that thin woman of twenty-four he was married to tell how to bring children up. Her lawyer, who wasn't much older, sat close enough to her to know when she was bouncing with rage. Then he put out a hand to silence her.

Her ex-husband's lawyer was the leader of the Children's Rights Movement. He had once been her son's camp counsellor. He looked nineteen.

She didn't like any of it at all. And it was going to be expensive. Like summer camp. Like school. Like limos. You can't, however, stop a course of treatment once you've started. You can't rely on yourself once you've been proved not to be good at it. Some children are special. You forge ahead. You pay.

Eighty dollars, eighty miles. She'd hear about this in court again if she sued for expenses. "She hires limousines." Walter looked like a kind old man. He wouldn't charge her all that much if . . . if he was willing to work for nothing. But the only people who work for nothing are mothers.

My God, she thought, I've developed a mind like an electronic calculator. It's only a book review and a bit.

The landscape went on being maddening. Nothing happened in it. Grey fields and grey-brown cornstalks and pink and grey sky. This was the plateau at the top of the escarpment. She'd been good at geography.

Her boy lay spread like a dead man: but correct. Uniform smooth and tie perfect. She ought to have bought him better shirts. Those enormous boots. It was a therapeutic school, military, and the boots were army boots. He was all feet and nose now, would get his growth later. All he had now was a combination of limpness and arrogance.

"Booorrrrring . . ." the boy said.

"You bet."

"Are we at Bismarck yet?"

"Mr Dunn says they're going to kill the TH and B."

"Know what it stands for?"

"Nope. I don't know anything."

"Toronto, Hamilton, and Buffalo. You know a lot."

He moaned and turned his white face to the seatback again.

There was another school, nicer, in Buffalo, but she had hesitated to send him over the border. He'd have hated anything, she said to herself. I had to send him away. They told me. We were all going mad. He'll never forgive me but at least he'll have something real never to forgive me for, not just feelings.

Walter cleared his throat. "You go right through Smithville," she said, "jog right, then left. Then on to Bismarck."

Smithville looked all right: a friendly white-frame and red-brick town, with a creek and a bridge. "There's the gross fish place," her son said.

"Soup is okay there."

"Yeah, I guess so. When Stratford's parents come they take him to . . ."

"I don't want to know. I have to come with other parents,

"Maybe we still do," she said evenly, furious with him.
"Look, I have to go out and see a man about a dog. If ten
dollars would do you, I could see you on your way."

"Drop me off somewhere?"

It wasn't the clothes he was wearing, it was the condition he
was in: tousled and dirty. "Ten bucks and a subway ticket.
That's it, Jack."

"You always were a tight old broad."

She went inside again, slamming the door, and pounded to
the front of the house so hard that the petals shivered off the
poppies she had set in a bowl in the front hall. She dashed upstairs and changed into another pair of trousers. As she went
down again she made sure the front door was locked, then the
back. "Here," she said, handing him ten dollars and a ticket.
"You can stay and finish your coffee. I have to be off." She
put her library book in her purse and strode off without looking behind her.

She was meeting Clive at the end of the subway line and
they were going out in the country to browse through antique
shops. That way he wouldn't have to drive downtown to her
place first. That way, she thought grimly, he avoided Jack,
thank God.

She had known him for only a few months and hadn't taken
him seriously at first. An ordinary man with an ordinary job,
he had seemed: indeed there was nothing special about him
except the fact that they got on together, very well indeed.
They were still in the wonderful time stage, however, and she
wondered vaguely if that would change. He was divorced,
and he had made it plain he wanted to set up housekeeping
with someone again. She didn't know whether she wanted to
live with anyone else: it had been so long since she hadn't had
the morning paper and the morning clock and the morning
coffee to herself that she was afraid she would resent an
intruder.

She saw him swing into the parking lot and smiled to herself. An intruder! He got out of the car and came towards her,
a smile on his face. He had a wide, rather shy smile, a funny

see, and we go where they choose.''

She'd rather liked the judge, a kind-looking woman in a blue dress. She felt in front of her that she didn't need to shriek and cry and say ''This shouldn't have happened.'' It wasn't good for the kid, it wasn't good for her. And there was his sister, who was somehow always left home alone while these bad things happened, to answer the phone. The time he got arrested the police said, ''And why weren't you home?'' She said, ''I was walking my daughter home from her ballet lesson past the filthy-picture houses.'' They hadn't been impressed.

Was he bad or mad or sad? He was bad now, sprawled out so in the huge car there was barely room for her. Bigfoot. What did he want? What would make life good for him, so he could function like other children? Military school, she'd been told. By three psychiatrists. They won the case, she didn't.

Children need love, her ex-husband had said desperately. Now she was broken, old. Love, what was that?

She had almost sent him alone. Walter looked reliable. But the school was new, miles from the old village it was nearest to, out on the river that came winding down from the Six Nations Reserve, isolated as can be. They got to Bismark and she told Walter to go straight on the gravel road. It was dark now.

Ages, it always was: only eighty miles and all of them a kind of Calvary, sending your boy away to those young men who looked like the cast of M.A.S.H. and seemed illiterate: and were fabulous friends and teachers, though you couldn't know that until later. Her ex-husband hated them on sight: she's giving my son away to them. So he sued. The school was new, had no reputation yet. It could have been Dotheboys Hall. Which her husband pronounced wrong in court.

''And what's happening,'' she wanted to ask the boy, ''who are we except you and me in white opposition, doing this expensive number. You've won: I've spent every cent I have to send you away and now I have to spend this extra, and brother, that's enough.'' But he wasn't her brother.

He was sitting up now. Young and keen and alert. Oh, lurch, she loved him. He had a beautiful profile: his father's. She liked his hair longer. They were nearly to the crossroads.

"Which way, ma'am?" Walter asked.

"Left," the boy cut in fast. "Left."

"Right," she said calmly.

Past the gas-station pop-stop where he'd been caught running away. Past the birdseed farm. The sign "To Bob and Ted's" was obliterated by the dark. But she remembered, because he wouldn't, that it was the first right after the level crossing. Then a hundred yards, and right to the dormitory, which looked like the old summer camp that it was.

The headmaster was waiting. "Say goodbye to your mother."

Whiter than ever, the boy shook her hand, then reached out. They held each other. "Bye," she said. "It ain't all that bad."

"Sure."

"Well," said the Head, "at least you won."

She wanted to say, Home, Walter, but she couldn't say anything like that ever again. She got into the front seat and told him the long sad story of her life. He didn't seem to mind.

Feet

A CHRISTMAS STORY FOR GROWN-UPS

Feet

A CHRISTMAS STORY FOR GROWN-UPS

Feet, Harris thought, feet.

The others were talking politics, regaling themselves with thoughts of Armageddon.

He was nearest the fire, drowsing over a brandy, detached from them. They were friends of Sara's. He didn't know them very well anyway. Two of the women were wearing Birken-stock sandals: German. The one cross-legged on the pillow in front of the fire had exquisite little nervous feet, narrow as documents. Their views didn't interest him; their feet, especially Sara's, tucked at the base of his spine and wiggling at the toes, did.

His father had left him the mill and it was his idea to have Christmas here. There was too much of Erika, his first wife, still left in his house. And if they were in the city there would be trouble with Mike.

Erika had never liked the mill; it was like his father, large and disorganized.

The people talking politics were Sara's friends, career women. Only one of them was married; her husband had already gone upstairs to bed so he could get up early and jog in the morning.

It was Christmas Eve, and in the background, miles, it seemed, from him and the fireplace, the children — his and hers, their lovers, their husbands — were dancing. Their music made Sara nervous, it sounded fascist to her, but he liked it.

He put a hand down onto the sofa and squeezed Sara's firm, fat little feet.

He often mused on the way he had met her or failed to meet her. She was his accountant for six months before he noticed her feet or her face or that she was female. It was just after Erika's death, and he was a walking puffball of self-pity. He was often grateful to the impulse that had led him to hold back. She might still suspect that the puffball was there, but she hadn't witnessed its most mawkish explosions. Unless he cried in his sleep.

Then one Thursday she didn't come in, and he found he missed her. When she returned, he looked at her carefully. She was short, stoutish, probably younger than she looked. She had small hands and feet and a bright eye like a bird's. "Were you ill?" he asked.

"In court."

"Nothing serious, I hope."

"My son."

"Pot?"

She shook her head, shrugged, started going down the figures again. "Joy-riding. He's at that age. The other boys stole the car."

"It could be serious."

"With Michael, it's always serious."

"Doesn't his father help?"

"Look, here's where you're out. You always make the same mistake, it must be because you're left-handed, you entered that zero too far over. His father's an alcoholic and I haven't seen him for years." In a flash, she corrected the error and snapped the book shut.

"Feel like coffee?"

"As a matter of fact, I do. I don't have to rush home tonight to see what Mike's up to: he's in a group home.''

In the restaurants they went to after that they talked about their more successful sons and daughters.

His had drifted away one by one after Erika's death, instinctively shaking the past away, leaving him alone in her beautiful house. When she was dying she had talked a lot about the things they had done together when they were young, savouring and storing the rich fruit of their time together. Now it seemed to hang decaying over his head: he liked to go out a lot.

Sara's time had been harder, though she had known no similar loss. She had come from a poor, hardworking family, flung herself into accounting when she was still a teenager, done brilliantly and found herself a charming wastrel to marry. ''Someone,'' she said, ''to take the edge off my compulsiveness.'' All through the raising of her children she had had to work, for her husband's charms included the inability to think in terms of providing for anyone but himself, and that poorly. Michael looked as if he were attempting to duplicate those charms, but it might just be a stage. ''I love the kid,'' she said, ''but I don't like him. I want him to find out now and not from me that if he breaks the rules he pays. Or he'll grow up like John, expecting other people to pick up the pieces.''

When he met the boy, he thought perhaps her judgment was unfair. After he had known him for six months and found himself lending money and advice, calling lawyers, intervening in school affairs and foolish contracts, he knew she was right.

When they decided to marry, his children, he was surprised to find, were indignant. They pulled reasons like rabbits from hats. ''She's too old.'' ''She's fat.'' ''That husband will come back and haunt you.'' ''Michael's awful.'' They were ugly.

''Jennifer,'' Sara said to his daughter, ''if I marry Daddy, you won't be able to, ever, will you?''

Harris was furious, but it worked. In a month, Jennifer was pleading for a double wedding.

He had taken his boots off when he came in from outside,

picking up brush for the fire. He stuck out his feet in their red health socks and stared at them. An absurd amount of him was turned under. He'd be a tall man, he thought, without these long feet. Sara wiggled her toes in his side.

"They're doing it in El Salvador, they're doing it in Uruguay and they did it in Chile. What side are we supposed to be on?" the young woman with the small feet said. Her name was Edme and she was, he thought, too pretty to be making political statements he had heard thirty years before. "Alice Sit-by-the-Fire," he murmured. She bristled and went to speak, closed her mouth, shrugged. He felt old and tired.

"Daddy," Jennifer called from the dancing end of the millhouse, "it's a slow one: come and dance."

"There," said Sara. "Go ahead. Somebody wants you!"

Her young people and his, with their absurdly formal polysyllabic names — Christopher, Jennifer, Alexandra, Michael, Nicholas, and Benjamin — were dancing in work socks or worn-out jogging shoes that looked oddly like bandages. The girls still had long hair like sheets and it swung around them as they danced, though the slow record had been taken off before he got his old bones as far as Jennifer and he was condemned to a thigh-wrenching version of the Charleston. When he was turned towards the fire he looked at it wistfully: the Christmas tree dreamed and gleamed in the corner where his father, the learned professor, had always put it. Christmas was the only time he had shared these quarters. In summer, the children went with their mother to the grandparents in Muskoka and the professor fished in books and the millrace all summer, alone. He wondered, in a brief gasp Jennifer gave him, if his parents had been happy. He was still unable to imagine their touching each other.

"Neat-o, Daddy, I didn't know you had it in you!" Jennifer released him and he reeled back to the sofa. Edme and one of the other women had gone out for a walk in the snow. Sara took his hand, "Well done for an old guy."

He was very tired. When he shut his eyes he seemed to be letting down old Venetian blinds on frayed cords. He thought of feet, feet, the feet that had marched through his life, the orthopaedic shoes of his mother's generation, his grandmother's kid shoes with silk laces, the saddle shoes and penny loafers of high-school girls, the pointed-heeled shoes they wore after that, the kind that got stuck in the lawn at graduation.

Storm-troopers' boots: he had had to have it out with Sara that Erika was German, that one could marry a German, because one married not a German but a pretty girl one loved. But there was always some small guilt attached to Erika, whom he had not loved quite enough, and it attached itself tonight to feet and tiptoed through the top of his head.

He drifted off for a moment and half woke thinking of summer feet in sandals, in sneakers, of girls who wore oxfords and walked like sailors and in summer went barefoot and came about and hauled a mean jib sheet. Erika had looked like one of those girls: tall, blonde and classic. It had been a disappointment to him that she was so European about nature. She had an absurd desire to tidy up the whole landscape of Canada. She was too clean and too orderly, he had found. Her feet were too thin. When she died she was only just over forty. If she had lived . . . would he have stayed with her? He felt guilty.

Sara poked him. "Hey, dreamer, here's a cup of coffee. Wake up, it's nearly midnight and Christmas is coming, remember?"

The music had changed. New Wave was replaced by a Bach cantata. Sara had put brandy in the coffee and built up the fire. Edme was back, saying, "Did your father really get this place at a tax sale?"

"The Dirty Thirties had another side."

"You could make a killing."

He shook his head. "It's on Crown land. It goes to the Heritage people when I go. Enjoy, enjoy."

Feet, yes, they were tied up with guilt somehow. This was his sour hour, the time when he needed to go to bed and couldn't; it was too early and he might wake up in an hour with insomnia. So legions of women's feet marched through his brain: Erika's, his mother's, his daughter's when she was held up after her birth, the inch-long feet of Jennifer Burden between the doctor's knuckles.

Feet. Later, not pitter-patter, but thud, thunk, wham.

Golf shoes, bowling shoes, track shoes, football shoes. The stairs groaning.

Feet. He was back there again, listening to the undertaker: "Dress, underclothing, stockings; you don't need to bring any shoes." Won't she be cold in her bare feet? he had wanted to ask. Then he had understood that she was dead.

Desperately: his father doing all the shoes on Saturday night, the First War veteran who knew how to make scuffed toe-caps shine. Green X-ray machines in Agnew Surpass, running in every day after school for a year to watch your toes wiggle, grey in a green outline. The wrong person got the cancer.

There was no reason he should not be tired. It had taken them two long days to get the mill warmed up, the plumbing operative, beds aired and made, floors clean. And tomorrow he had promised to do the cooking, for it was the Burden men who had mastered this woodstove. He hoped.

Sara, deep in conversation with Anne and Barbara and Edme, wiggled her toes in his thigh. He fought down the feeling that he was lost in his own bulk, stuck in the past, unable to pull forward. Christmas always does it, he thought. He wondered if he ought to get up and offer more drink, but no, this wasn't a drinking crowd like the old one; too many had fallen by the wayside.

Over in the corner, Jennifer and Nicholas were dancing to the Bach. They were both in jeans and huge Irish sweaters, thin as skeletons. There must be something in all that alfalfa he thought. And began to feel better.

"You're tired," Sara said, mothering him.

"Aren't you?"

"You bet. I'd have been in bed an hour ago if . . . thank God we didn't offer Rick and Edme ours!"

"I'm good, but not that good."

"The kids are getting along well."

"Michael's been really amusing tonight."

"Hey! It's midnight." She slung an arm on his shoulder and kissed him.

The record had been turned off and the mill was suddenly hushed. Something is going to happen, he thought, but what? At midnight at Christmas there is mass if you are Catholic, supper and candles on the tree if you are with Erika, but with us? What can happen on Christmas Eve when I am thinking about death?

Suddenly, the front door opened as if it had been blown in by the wind. Against the white yard and the stand of birch trees, three crowned figures stood in tableau.

The tallest, garbed in a striped bathrobe held together with a bony hand, moved forward carrying a box wrapped in gold-coloured paper. "Blessed are the feet of him who bringeth good tidings," he said. "Merry Christmas," the two others chorused, rushing in, breaking the unity, slamming the frozen air out. One carried a pineapple, one an enormous orange. "Merry Christmas, Dad and Mum." Dumping their largesse in their laps.

Harris and Sara opened their first Christmas present jointly and carefully. It was a large and beautifully sewn banner, with the six children's names incorporated in a design of birds and boats and flowers. "For the mill," they said breathlessly. "Alex designed it and Jennie did most of the sewing but we all worked on it. It's for the mill. So you'll have to have us here forever and ever!"

Before Harris could think of anything to say, from the depths of the mill the old pump-organ began to wheeze. He could see a huge pair of jogger's feet squeezing the sound out. "Silent Night," they all began to sing. "Holy night."

Michael's voice floated out, high, clear, sweet, and beautifully in tune. They let him finish alone. Sara hugged Harris and cried a little.

When the moment was over, the young people bundled up

again to go and make angels in the virgin snow, leaving Harris and Sara together in the corner of the sofa holding each other. The guests simply disappeared. The mill was so quiet that he could almost feel his stippled white Christmas beard growing.

"I have hope," Sara whispered. "I have hope." Harris made a pattern of kisses on the top of her head.

Hours later, when they had all been packed away on beds and couches in bags and blankets, he woke and heard the water in the millrace, the mice in the walls. He remembered where the warmest bit of floor was over the stove-pipe, he remembered exactly which uncle had endowed the mill with a striped Christmas-king's bathrobe. He remembered that he had loved Erika once as he loved Sara beside him now. He remembered that it was sage and sausage-meat his father put in the turkey dressing. Sara rolled against him. He remembered her feet. He smiled. He fell asleep.

Anita's Dance

Anita's Dance

It was a morning fit to convert any pessimist, and a Sunday to boot. Anita spent part of it in the garden virtuously weeding; then she poured enough coffee to float an army into her special mug and brought it out into the garden. Instead of reading, she sat stretching her neck to the sun and thinking how lucky she was: nothing to do but please herself all day. From time to time friends lectured her about being selfish and set in her ways, an old maid. And it was true she was sometimes lonely. She had, however, no reason to feel sorry for herself when she compared her life to theirs. She had a house, a garden, a car, a piano. A good job. A greedy, bad-tempered cat. Two eyes, a nose, and ten fingers, all in good working order. What did she have to feel sorry about? And was happiness selfish?

She mused over her library book. She had never really wanted to get married, except for a brief and embarrassing episode when she was at university. A boy she was very fond of had wanted her to drop her scholarship, marry him and put him through law school. Her fondness had ceased abruptly when he argued that, being male, he had more right to an education than she had. Winning the argument had hurt a lot.

Those days were over, she thought, and if she was wrong, she had no daughter to tell her so in exemplary form. I have my house, she thought, my garden with delphiniums and daisies and poppies. My piano, on which I have taught myself to play the simplest and saddest waltzes of Chopin. I have company in the form of a bad-tempered cat. What is more, I have a date with Clive this afternoon. I feel good with Clive. The something that is between us is nothing: there is no self-consciousness. We swim towards each other as if the water were our element. All's right with the world.

She had wanted to study literature but on practical grounds had chosen economics instead. She still, however, attempted to keep up with good books and now she was reading a novel by a man in England called Berger, who was supposed to be both good and avant garde. She opened it now, and put on her sun-glasses.

It was good: his main characters were small souls, which showed a sort of left-wing point of view, but she liked the way he got into both their heads at once and managed to stay there, so she could feel both the room they were in and the beating of their rather constricted hearts.

It took place in a small employment agency; both characters, the owner and his clerk, were weighing large changes in their private lives while appearing to deal with clients. The owner, a fiftyish man who had always lived with his sister, was considering independence: marriage even.

She looked up and smiled at the sun. That was funny. She read on.

A woman came into the agency to look for a housekeeping job. A largish, comfortable, middle-aged woman. The proprietor had an instant vision of the comfort she could provide for him: a well-kept house — not too well-kept, Canadian and mowed in the lawn departments, just a sort of comfy English house, fish and chips for tea, a kettle on the hob.

"I could live with that," Anita said to herself. "What I couldn't live with, not ever, is a set-up like this plus a job, plus three children and entertaining for a junior executive now portly and senior. No wonder I'm the way I am.''

She frowned at the book, closed it, and put it down. It had revealed to her a seam of domesticity she had been avoiding recognizing: it was cosy, and it was basically English working class, and basically (except for a mob of children) what she had come from.

She had never wanted her mother's life, one of flying elbows and fits of bad temper and aspirations that were a muddle of impulses. Her mother had never seemed to be able to think anything through, she was always anaemic from childbearing and exhausted from scrubbing; crying out ''You girls . . .'' Get this, fetch that, turn off the soup, scrub the sink, do the dishes, iron that. When she was an old woman they had bought her an automatic washing machine with a window in the door and found her sitting on the basement steps watching it like television. ''I was remembering the day Lanie got her hair caught in the wringer,'' she said.

Anita shuddered: that dream of cosy domesticity was a male dream; she'd been living in a man's world too long. The real thing she'd lived through and it was what had made her so happy to get a scholarship to university. Never mind that she'd had to char and work in a grocery store to put herself through.

She stretched lazily. The cat was scowling at her through the kitchen window; he didn't like her to be happy. Too bad for him. She was going to enjoy this day. Clive and she weren't meeting until two and she didn't even have to change.

She heard scuffling footsteps on the gravel, the footsteps of her brother Jack. ''Oh damn,'' she thought. ''He's found me.''

''Hi Nita, how's tricks?''

''Where did you come from, Jack?''

He was big, and he was stupid, something of a bad dream: the one who hadn't succeeded. ''Oh well, you know,'' he said, plunking himself down on the chaise longue so it clicked and shivered. "I was wondering if you had any jobs for me, like."

"Broke again, eh? Want some coffee?"

"Sure."

She slammed the kitchen door as she went in. The cat gave her a satisfied look, pleased that her moment of glory was over. She poured Jack a coffee, creamed and sugared it, and stumbled as she went out, staining her white summer pants. "Here," she thrust it at him.

He sat up like a patient in bed and began not so much to drink as to inhale it. He looked badly hung over. "What have you been doing lately?" she asked.

"I been doing . . . well, littla this, littla that. Delivering leaflets. You know."

She knew. He was no good, Jack, and that was that.

"I keep up with the work around here myself," she said. "I don't really have anything for you to do."

"There must be something, the way you lie around reading all the time."

She refused to rise to the bait.

"Lanie's poorly," he said. "I was there yesterday."

He must be making the rounds again, she thought, borrowing from all of us.

"She's got cancer," he said, almost with satisfaction: the voice of the child at school announcing family bad news for current events class. "She looks awful, and she can hardly move."

"She's doing all right," Anita said.

"Gotta get worse before you get better eh? I don't think she'll get better. Ross is scared out of his wits. You should take the kids."

"I can't. I go out to work, remember?"

"I remember," he said and continued to stare at her, trying to put her in the wrong before he asked her for money.

"I wrote to Rosie but she's just had an operation. Kit's on the sick list too. Bill won't open the door to me. In the old days, a family stuck together."

walk. "Hi," she said, and ran towards him. "Marvellous day."

"Wonderful." He put her into the car like the gentleman he was, said, "Belt up, now," and headed north.

Ordinarily, this act of merely strapping herself in beside him made her happy, but today it was different. Jack niggled and danced in her mind. Being mean to Jack made her feel like the mean, ignorant child she no doubt had been, that Jack still was.

"What's the matter?" Clive said. "You're twitchy."

"I'm mean-tempered today," she said. "As bad as Martha the cat. My brother Jack turned up. The no-good one."

"You have one of those, have you? Most people do. I always used to wonder why they felt sorry for me for being an only child. How much did you give him?"

So that was on her face too. He read her well. "I was having such a good time," she said, "reading in the garden. Then in stomped Jack, and I still feel shattered."

"Whom were you reading?"

"John Berger."

"I'm always amazed at your taste: hardly anyone's heard of him. Look, about your brother, you'd better tell me about him and get it off your mind. No use having a day in the country if we're not in good spirits. Was he mother's blue-eyed boy?"

Suddenly she heard her mother yell, "You girls, Nita, Rosie, look after that Jackie and make sure he don't fall in the well." She hunched herself and said, "First, you have to understand we were small-town people and not what you'd call well off." She had used the genteel phrase for so long it didn't surprise her any more.

"Born with a plastic spoon?"

"Tin. My father was a sergeant in the army."

"Powerful influence?"

"When he was there. There were four girls, then Jackie and Bill. Jackie tore the wings off flies and drowned our kitten in the rain barrel: we hated him. I'm sure he was disturbed or something, but I don't bleed for him; he was an awful kid and he's an awful man.''

''I was a social worker in my first incarnation,'' he said, profile to the wind against a blue and scudding sky. ''No good at it, but I met a lot of them, awful boys who never grew up. I suppose they radicalized a lot of big sisters in their day. How often has he been inside?''

''I suppose three or four times: petty theft, drunkenness, nothing big or skilful. We were no help to him, you know. He needed a lot of attention from adults, not sisters who'd rather be doing something else.''

''Don't flog yourself, for heaven's sake. There are bad apples, and handing them the barrel doesn't help. Where is he now?''

''In my backyard on the chaise, I suppose. I gave him ten bucks and a subway ticket. But there's no real hope he's gone yet.''

Clive looked at her and slowed the car down. ''I think,'' he said, ''that we'd better go back . . .''

''Clive, I don't want to spoil your day in the country.''

''You're more important than a day in the country and you're miserable. And that oaf is probably inside drinking the liquor cabinet: you can't win with those guys, Nita.''

''I locked the doors.''

''He's probably got Martha to open up for him by now; come on.''

He turned the car and drove very fast down the half-empty Sunday highway into town. They were home in twenty minutes.

They went in the front door and found Jack reclining with his work boots on the white corduroy sofa. He was drinking Nita's precious duty-free French cognac from her last trip to Europe from a kitchen glass.

''Jack!'' she roared.

''Snob,'' he said with an impish smile. ''So you caught me, you and your fine feller here. Nice coat he's got on. You're coming up and up and up in the world, aren't you, girl? Ma would be proud of you." But he swung his boots off the chesterfield.

"I think you'd better go," Clive said. "You're bothering Anita."

"Do you think so, Mr Prettyboy? What are you doing hanging around our Nita? Don't you know she's our Educated Woman, too good for a man? Why, all she cares about is white velvet and books and doilies. She don't even go to visit the sick and the dying, she . . ." He spoke in a stage Irishman's accent. Anita's blood began to rise and she could hear children in the background chanting, "Nita's a nitwit, Nita's a nobody . . ."

"Jack," she said. "Get out."

"And why would I want to get out, with a fine house to come to and a fine sister to look after me?"

"You should go," said Clive, being reasonable, trying, being also, Anita thought, very sweet and middle class, "because your sister has asked you to go."

"Oh, I never did nothing Nita told me. It was Rosie had the good left hook. Nita was nothing, all skin and bone and no bust. No wonder she never got married or nothing. But then you wouldn't be so foolish, mister, would you, as not to open a package before you put it on the shelf?" His mouth turned down and he leered at Clive. He stood up and prepared to raise the bottle to his lips.

On the one hand, Anita wanted to laugh because he was being a self-defeating grotesque, asking for punishment, exile, anything: he had always been like that. But she was also very, very angry. She could hear all the fourteen-year-old boys in the world whispering, "Nita Nobody, got no tits . . ." and the rest of it, which was worse. The rest of us reclaimed ourselves, she thought, as Mother wanted us to. We got out of misery and brutality. We stopped swearing, read books, got at least a smattering of education: cleaned up the family act.

Jack took a swig from the bottle. Clive balled his fists. Nita looked at the two of them and sized them: Clive was taller, but Clive was nervous. Clive had never had to punch anyone out.

Jack put the bottle down. Nita took his measure and lashed out, one two, one two, and bang bang bang on his falling head with her fists. Jack went down like a lamb.

Nita sat down on the sofa and started to cry. Clive sat down beside her and put his arm around her. Jack came to.

"Nita, you shouldn't ought to have done that. Nita, you damn well broke me false teeth."

"Get out, Jack," she said. "Get flaming well out of this house and don't come back. If you don't, or if you ever come back, I'll flaming well . . . I'll call your probation officer."

Jack stood up, holding his head, trying again. "Nita, you're a hard woman. You should know," he said to Clive, "this is the kind of woman you're after: she's got no heart, she's all hollow."

"Shut up, Jack, and go and tell your government psychiatrist you're persecuted by your sister," Nita said. "Get out. Get on with you. Go home and tell your mother she wants you."

He went.

Anita sat trying to pull herself together. In the scuffle she had lost more than a lamp: the brandy bottle oozed on the carpet, the glass was broken. She sat up and sighed. She looked at Clive.

"Well," she said. "Now you know."

Clive got up and reappeared with a cloth. He began sponging the brandy out of the carpet. "Look," he said, "there's something I should tell you, but I want to know first how you did that?"

"What?"

"That wonderful kayo; I've never seen anything like it."

"I wasn't born a lady and a scholar," she said. "I was born on the outskirts of Camp Borden, a longer time ago than you were, I have to come clean and tell you that. I was one of six children. Circumstances were not good. But in addition to being a sergeant, my father was a fighter, and when he got a beer or two into him he'd spar with anyone he could find. We saved my mother a lot.''

Clive disappeared for a moment again. She picked up the fallen glass, looked at herself in the mirror, smoothed down her hair. Thought desperately: now he knows. It's over.

Clive reappeared with a tray and glasses. ''It's our turn for a drink. There's something I said I would tell you, and I will. The real reason my wife and I got divorced was boredom. We never got quite so low as Graham Greene, who had a tooth out once when he couldn't stand it any more. But we got bored in a terrible way; we got so bored we felt we needed some kind of violence; we knew it wasn't for us, but we started to pick fights because we drove each other crazy. All our friends celebrated when they heard we were getting a divorce. Perfection drives everybody up the wall.''

She managed to look up at him and smile.

''So drink up, love. I don't care what happens between us; I know it won't bore me. But if we ever do take up living together and things get all sedate and cosy, would you . . .''

''I'd do anything for you,'' she heard herself say, not believing she had said it, but hearing it anyway.

''Well, I'm not really that way, but . . . well, hell, Nita: you're magnificent in the boxing ring.''

Much later he said, after tangling with her, ''It wasn't that I wanted violence: I wanted a feeling that I was alive, that you were alive, that even our hair was growing.''

She smiled at her professor again and rubbed her bruised hands together.

The Confession Tree

Timor Mortis Conturbat Ne

The Confession Tree

Timor Mortis Conturbat Ne

Mary Abbot was standing at the back door staring at the apple tree in the garden, which just that morning had burst into bloom. She tried to stare hard enough at it to be swallowed by, to enter into, that cloud of pink and white unreality. It was an old tree, and it gave her pleasure every year it survived.

Mary Abbot's mother, Mrs Beatty, was standing at the ironing board, pressing Osborne's no-iron shirts, and talking to herself.

Since she had come home from the hospital, Mary sometimes found the gears in her mind slipping, as if her father's movie projector was running backwards and she was a child again, rising from an untidy splash backwards like a bent hairpin to the smooth rock they dived off: plump and pigtailed and proud for him. Or even smaller, saying to herself, I went into the hospital well and came home sick.

I must stop that, she thought. That's madness. I went into the hospital thinking I was well, and they found it. I'm taking my bottom to an elbow specialist again; I've got to get a grip on myself.

Her mother talked serenely on, as she would to the end of her days. Mary pretended she was talking about Mr

McGregor's garden: alas, it was a newer story, though not one she hadn't heard before.

"That Osborne," she was saying, "the way he takes advantage of you, Mary. Untidy, crumpling his newspapers onto the floor as he reads them . . ."

"He stopped that years ago, Mother . . ."

"Never picks up after himself, never helps around the house, never home."

"He's upstairs with his computer, Mother."

"He might as well be in Mars."

As he might indeed be, and Mary was angry with him for it, buying a computer to spend his sabbatical with when she was in the hospital.

"Wasting his money. Not that he hasn't a lot of it, those Abbots, and his stepfather was a Jew, wasn't he? You living in this rich neighbourhood and him treating you like a servant . . ."

"That's enough, Mother." They had had this out before. If Mrs Beatty wished to sleep under Osborne's roof, she was expected to be loyal to Osborne. She had finally understood this after three years' banishment from the household.

But she was old now, and she did what she wanted. The day after Mary had come home, she had turned up at the front door with a man who had found her lost in the bus station. Mary had wanted to burst into tears, and the nice man had delivered her a little homily about taking care of your parents. So she was here until she could be persuaded to go home to her neat little apartment in the north, or to one of her other daughters, and being as bad as she could be.

"I told you years ago never to marry a man whose mother had a maid, but you wouldn't listen, not you, Mary."

Mary drifted again into the cloud of the apple tree. Most years when it burst into bloom she invited her friends to lunch under it. They would drink white wine with her and tell her the most astonishing things, the delicate whorl over their heads opened their spirits, they revealed their loves, their hates. One had advised Mary to take better care of her figure so that Osborne would never leave her, and then been left herself, and committed suicide. Another had announced with viciousness that she hated her husband, and stayed with him. "This year there's nobody to play with," Mary thought. "They've all gone back to work." And another thought seeped through from another level, maybe there won't be a next year. I want it now, she thought: lunch under the tree. That cloud of odd revealing happiness.

"He's so inconsiderate: buying that expensive machine to play games on."

"He's programming it for his logic course, Mother."

"He's programming it to play war games with Henry."

They say you live longer if you keep your spirits up, Mary thought. That's what that Nomi woman said. You keep your blood count up by keeping your spirits up. You think pure thoughts. You send your white blood cells in like warriors.

"I'd fight, if I were you," Mrs Beatty said. "I'd tell him he can't have the thing in the house. Fancy, a grown man spending all his time with a toy."

What if I yelled at her, Mary wondered. What if I said what I'm thinking: I don't want you here with your meanness, your childish wickedness. You're standing there doing useless work, with a smug reproachful look because you know I'm a useless woman: I don't knit, I never iron, and I do what I darn well please. And I'm happy when you're not here, I'm darned well happy. Except about that computer.

"Mother," she said, "I think we'll have lunch outside under the tree. There's some shrimp in the fridge."

"It's a bit cold outside. I'd like to eat in here. And a little ham would do me fine."

Mary dug in the cupboard and found a tin of salmon. As it whirred on the electric can opener she thought, you can go on if you're happy, but that can't be right: lots of happy people die of it. Dodie wasn't unhappy and she went in six months. It must be true what the doctor says: it's all luck and chemotherapy.

"Inside," said Mrs Beatty firmly. "Is that Osborne coming down?"

I shall make myself a wig of apple petals. "Outside, Mother, the weather's beautiful. Shut up the ironing board.

I've made us a salmon sandwich.''

"I can't eat brown bread.''

"Yes you can, and the roughage is good for you.''

"There's a breeze, I'll get a bad back if I sit in a draught.''

"You sat in a draught all the way from Kapuskasing and you're just fine now.''

She helped the poor gnarled old knuckles put up the ironing board (''It was dusty, Mary.'') and untie the apron straps. She found the cardigan. She took a bottle of white wine out of the fridge, found the opener, set up garden chairs, trays and plates of the little conventional lunches her mother used to make at home: a sandwich with the crust cut off, a bright green chemical pickle, a stick of celery. She had no tomato aspic.

She helped her mother down the steps. Poor frail thing that once lived in a teacherage in the mountains and slept with her vegetables to keep them from freezing: stoked the stove, hauled the water, kept big boys in line, married a miner.

"Oh, are we having wine? Is it that mild wine that Osborne gets from France?'' It was no longer necessary to be teetotal.

"I always celebrate when the tree comes out.''

"The apples are wormy, aren't they?''

"There's something wrong with them: they have brown spots inside. They're a job to pick up in the fall, but I dig them into the beds.''

"Isn't Osborne coming?''

"He likes to work six hours at a stretch. He gets his own lunch when he's through.''

"I don't know how you could marry such a dry stick of a man. No wonder Henry's difficult: he needs a real father. All that money and not a drop of warm blood in his body.''

"Now, Mother.'' No point in saying that all that money was invested in City of Toronto debentures that didn't mature until 1990 (will I see them? will I see them?) at three percent. No use riding against the legend, better to ride against your disease. "Have some more wine, Mother. Is your sandwich all right?''

"Well, I would have preferred white bread. My, I do like it here. I must say, your house is comfortable. It's warmer than Kapuskasing."

"It was a strange place to retire. Why did you?"

"Oh, your father would have been a fish out of water in the south, Mary. You're the only one of the family ever went south. My, when the company said they'd send the engineers' children to boarding school because there was only the convent at Val d'Or within reach, you jumped at the chance. You got on that train and turned away from us and left without looking back."

Mary had heard this before too, visualized and imagined and remembered every moment of the trip: leaving home for the first time at twelve. And she saw them all on the platform, standing straight and tall with their church-look on their faces; Mother, Father, two sisters (Betty was training for a nurse in Winnipeg) and beside her in the carriage of the train (at what station? what line was it?) Berthille Lapointe in hysterics because she was going to Sacre Coeur in Montreal and the nuns stuck the children with hatpins. "Hey, Bertilla, come off it, pull yourself together." Stooping to hold Berthille together and missing her own goodbyes.

I shouldn't have given her that wine, Mary thought. She'll talk more. And inside, the voice of her deepest panic snarled "Honour thy father and thy mother that thy days may be long . . ."

She knew how the story would go on: "And you never looked back. You stayed south and finished high school. You went to university — my, we had a job paying for that and you were only taking Secretarial Science — and then you got that good job in Europe and you married a rich man. Oh, I guess he's good to you," — a titter closing the mouth — "if he's a professor at the university at least he earns your living . . ." There was nothing and would be nothing in her mother's life as good as a mining engineer, a man who hacked his living out of rock.

It was true, she supposed, that she was a snob in her

mother's eyes. She liked cities and theatre and concerts. She hated being cold. The north was all right if you liked hockey and skiing and could face the Legion Hall and bingo. But you had to belong to the old mould and find your satisfactions in handicraft and an infinite variety of housework. You had to like sports and carpentry and hobbies. You couldn't get books, and there weren't any movies. Probably television had saved all their winters from madness. It was a good life for a different sort of person, which Mary wasn't, the little snob.

I was her baby, Mary thought, and I left her.

Her mother was silent for a moment. Something, the precious orange gleam of an oriole in the branches, the wine, the possibility of bringing Mary yet again to bay had stopped her.

She lay back in her chair, crossed her ankles, raised her face to the tree and closed her eyes. "Corinne Dunton's gone," her mother said. "Of course, she was French."

These days, she was obsessed by remembering. It was as if it was her job, her Christian mission. Everything had to come back. She was at once in a square in Teheran twenty years ago meeting Osborne for the first time, in London at some peculiar non-ceremony (who had given her the flowers?) marrying him, and here, coming to this house for the first time.

That's right, they had come in from the airport in a taxi and gone down Bay Street to a lawyer's office where they were greeted very gravely and given the keys. Then they had taken another taxi, Osborne all the while greyer and grimmer and saying, "Well, I don't think you'll find it's much," and "They may have neglected it totally," and "I suppose we can still go to the Village for food." She was hunched up and puzzled and afraid for herself, because she knew it was not only a house they were going to but the abode of some dark thing inside himself. The part of Osborne that was not puzzled by sun and reality lived here, and it might be a different man she was with when they stepped in the door.

It was a good house, she saw at once when the taxi drew up,

on a good street: one of a row with pretensions to Tudor half-timbering, but fairly old, from the thirties. The sort of house her boarding-school friends had come from: middling prosperous, but not rich. One of the ornamental trees had spread itself right across the front walk. Other than that there was nothing special about it. The windows were made of little leaded lozenges, and they were clean.

Osborne was nervous. He dropped his change when he paid the taxi driver, and he dropped his keys. His hands shook as he opened the door. "There," he said, swinging it open, a brown door with silly English-looking studs and a little barred window. "At least it's ours." He didn't carry her over the doorstep and she was glad.

She stepped inside solemnly. The furniture was all shrouded in sheets, and as Osborne flicked the light switch a little puff of dust sprang up and flowed into a beam of light from the oriel window on the stairs.

The house had been shut for three years, ever since Mrs Thompson the housekeeper died. There were no cobwebs, but a fine layer of dust lay everywhere. It was warm and light, but oddly like the inside of a tomb, and as she went through the living-room to the dining-room she expected to find the big table laid out with Miss Havisham's feast. She looked around in wonder. "It's a lovely house, Osborne."

"Ill-gotten gains," he shrugged.

Together they began to strip the sheets from the furniture, rolling them up to contain their dust, revealing two fine serpentine sofas, oval Victorian tables, stuffy sidechairs and armchairs. "Your grandmother had taste," she said.

"I don't remember her. She was dead when I came here. I was five."

She knew that his father had been one of the first casualties of the Second World War. She knew that his mother had had to return home to care for his father. She knew that he had grown up in this house. "It's all yours," he said. "Do what you want with it. Apparently there's lots of money."

The money was there, but not a fortune, and tied up in debentures. She had not been able to strip the panelling, bleach the floors, replace the silly lozenge windows. She had merely, as the children arrived, moved the best of the furniture upstairs to their bedroom and Osborne's study and felt exotic as she lay nursing her babes on the beautiful serpentine sofas. The house was big and shabby and comfortable now, and, not having been teased and twisted into something it wasn't, it bore its age gracefully. Even the black and white tiled bathrooms were back in fashion again. She had put her energy into the garden because Osborne didn't care what he ate, didn't notice food, disliked colour on the walls, hated noise. It was the children who made the house alive.

"Perce Norman has cancer," her mother said. Which of the treacherous children had mentioned the disease to her? Which one knew? Emma, perhaps, who could read lips.

"It's a pathetic thing. He's a skeleton. He can hardly walk. Do you remember him, Mary? He used to go fishing with Dad. They'd put a canoe on the train — Perce was an engineer but not on that line — on their holidays and they'd get the fellow to slow down on a curve by a lake they liked the look of, throw the canoe off, jump down themselves and fish until the crew came back for them. Oh, I was fit to be tied when I heard that."

"I liked him. He was a nice man."

"He certainly was. And a big man, too. You wouldn't believe him to see him now: he looks as if he's been hollowed out."

"Is Mrs Norman still alive?"

"Oh, of course. But she has a hard, hard time of it with him. She's just a little bit of a thing, and the VON comes to help her turn him in bed. But, oh, Mary, they took him down to Sudbury to give him the cobalt and she says what it's done to his skin . . ."

Suddenly the oriole, undeterred by the buses on Bathurst Street, started to sing. "Excuse me, Mother, I must just get a cardigan, I'm cold."

Mary ran upstairs to the bathroom and vomited. Then she cleaned herself up and wandered distracted around the upstairs hall, opening and shutting doors and drawers, expecting skulls to fall out of the linen closet, burn bandages on doorknobs. Osborne's computer whirred and she thought she heard him humming and she wanted to pound on the door and yell at him, but she couldn't think what, except, "I need you," which in front of her mother she could hardly do. And the interior voice wasn't saying anything, it was making a noise like a bad drain instead.

But she would have to go back or explain where she had been: you can't deconstruct an old woman's world. She wandered into Henry's room and saw on his dresser a battery-operated tape recorder with earphones that he had been forbidden to take to school. She seized it and rushed down to the living-room, found music, slotted it in, put the earphones on her head and went outside.

Her mother was still talking. She could lip-read too, they all could, because Emma was deaf and had taught them. So she turned away from Mrs Beatty, away from the accounts of disease and disaster that are so reassuring to the elderly, and let the rush of Schubert in her ears pour out through her eyes into the apple tree. All the voices stopped, and there was only music and this benison of blossom.

Eventually she felt a tap on her knee, heard the back door slam. There was Osborne, smiling. He came right up to her and turned the tape recorder off. "You've got that vacant look Henry wears when he's listening."

"I should think so."

"Osborne," said Mrs Beatty smiling, "you've come to join us at last."

"Not for long, Ma Beatty," he said. "It's back to work for sinners. But that was Betty on the phone: she wants you to fly home tomorrow. There's a reservation if you're up to it."

Mrs Beatty gave him her special sweet smile. "Well, aren't you all thoughtful. Are you sure it would be convenient to take me to the airport?"

"Flight's at ten: there'll be lots of work time after that. Mary, you look tired. Why don't you and your mother go and have your naps. I'll finish the wine and clear up here." He gave her a wink and picked up their plates and trays. "That way you'll be fresh when Henry rushes in and accuses you of stealing his property."

Mary helped her mother to bed almost tenderly. We loved each other once, she thought, before we headed for different men. Or were we always competing for the same one?

At suppertime Osborne was unwontedly jolly and insisted they have wine, and play guessing games. Georgie won, of course, and Henry went off in a funk. Emma and her grand-mother loaded the dishwasher together because they were best friends. Mary blessed the stars that Emma's young man with the blue eyelids was not around that night.

Driving home from the airport, Osborne said. "I phoned Betty."

"I'm glad you did. I was going out of my mind. She knows when I'm mad at you. She, I don't know how to put it, she grooves into my negatives like a needle on a record player. I hate that computer, Osborne. You're there and not there."

"You'll get used to it, I hope. I can't keep it at the univer-sity. And Henry likes it. I know what you mean about her and there's not much you can do, Mary, I need it desperately for my work, you know that. It extends the possibilities enor-mously."

She felt like sulking again, but the day was too bright so she smiled and he stroked her neck. "Hard lines," he said, "your ma turning up at the door so soon."

As they got out of the car he peered into the backyard over his glasses and said, "Let's have lunch out under the tree. Do we need more wine? I'll go and get some."

She put together a picnic — it was a great advantage to have a husband who didn't care what he ate — and when he came back she was shaking off yesterday's chairs. Osborne stared up into the whorling blossom and said, "My grandfather was like that. That's not bad wine, plonk, really, but either my palate's degenerated or they're doing it better. Sit close to me, Mary. I'm cold with memory, and I need you.

"They go mad with jealousy, you know. They're afraid of dying and they see us here with our youth, our future all before us. They can't understand that we're middle-aged and frightened too. We're still their children, dashing off into the future without looking behind us, and that with unsuitable companions. He used to shake his cane at the synagogues going up and yell that they were building heathen temples. He roared at the heathen jazz music on the radio. He wouldn't let Mother go out alone at night. He gave her a dollar a week allowance and me ten. I used to take her out to quite unsuitable places."

She had heard some of this before, but the version was new and passionate. The oriole started to sing again. "There haven't been orioles for years," she said.

"The pollution must be getting better. It was rage," he said, "rage that he suffered from. He had to give it all up and die, and leave it to us: it made him hate us. He might even have thought he was going to hell. Where was the forgiveness in the old preacher's thunderations? He must have had sinful thoughts: he'd get up in the night and yell the most dreadful obscenities outside my mother's door. I had school to go to and my books to hide in, but he nearly drove her insane. Then when he found she was going out with Sam Bernstein the fur really flew. When I turned sixteen we sneaked out to dinner and I saw them off for Palm Beach at the Union Station."

"I thought she drank."

"Oh, she did, some of the time. She couldn't do anything else. She'd lock herself in her room with bottles of ghastly sherry. I didn't mind when she went. Though it was lonely. I used to write my own notes for school. 'Please excuse Osborne who was up all night reading Wittgenstein.' Kids can survive anything."

But can I? she wondered.

"Most of the time he was all right after she left. They're better with grandchildren than children. When he was bad and batty I just ignored him. I took his car keys and taught myself to drive. That old Chrysler was a heavy machine. Mrs Thompson cooked for us and I guess she talked to him during the day. Sometimes at night he wandered and raved and fell out of bed. He'd come into my room and roar about hellfire and venereal disease.''

''Somebody told me you used to study in the reading room of the Granite Club.''

''The Toronto Club. Until Senator Brown caught me smoking a cigar. If you can't be a person, you can be a character. I must have felt lost. I don't remember. I wore his Homburg so I'd look older and it worked: the police never caught me for not having a driver's licence.

''He died. I've told you about that before, how he died. It seemed a miracle that he could actually come to a stop at the end of that long slide. He died saying, 'I fought a good fight' and he believed it. And he left me the house and money to go to Oxford. But, oh, Mary, I never had anything until I had you.''

She stared at him. His hair was receding now. He was tall and thin and white and his odd high forehead looked as vulnerable as an eggshell. Still.

The Smell of Sulphur

The Smell of Sulphur

There were two girls in that family, Tess and Janie, six years apart. Tess was the little one, named after her mother's cousin Maria Theresa Brown, who worked at *The Toronto Star* and gave her namesake a silver locket. Only Theresa was a Catholic name and wouldn't do, so she was called Tessa Marie. She was six that summer and Janie was twelve. Janie called her Tillie the Toilet, after the comic character and her own feelings.

What happened was that when their father went to his ulcer doctor in Brantford in March, the doctor said, "Frank, you've still got that house-on-wheels thing of yours, and when school lets out in June, I tell you what you're going to do and it isn't a suggestion, it's an order. There's a place called Star Bay about five miles from my cottage up the Bruce. All the land there is owned by a family named Ellis and I know them well. Nobody much is going up there now because of gas rationing, and what you're going to do is save up your gas ration, drive up there and park your trailer where the hotel used to be and spend two months fishing."

Frank went back later and was told that a man who taught

boys to fix cars wouldn't have a hard time laying hands on a boat: they'd needed a mechanic up there the last ten years. The two men talked bass and pickerel and glowed.

Maudie got out the sewing machine and started running up seersucker outfits for Tessa. Janie ordered hers from Eaton's catalogue, she was that age.

Tessa had few talents, and her greatest one was being sick in the car. Once it was over with, Janie was the one who suffered. Tessa sat high in the back seat of the Studebaker Commander, Queen of the World as the landscape rushed by her, changing at her command. The trailer had, her father said, the best hitch in Christendom, and, her mother said, this made them snails with their house on their back. Tessa looked and smiled and babbled and nobody listened. Janie practised her Deanna Durbin imitations.

It took a long time to get there, and where was that? First the road was all farms, then it was cottages with bits of lake glistening between them, but that wasn't where they were going. They entered a flat, desolate landscape, where there were grey stones and sheep and scrubby bushes. The road was very straight. There wasn't any traffic: they were the only ones who had been provident enough to save their whole gas ration. You had to hand over a coupon the way you had to for butter, but they were a different colour and shape. It was about the war, but Tessa didn't care: the day the King came on everyone had looked serious and told her not to talk in competition with the radio.

"Now girls, look out," their mother, Maudie, said from the front seat. She had black hair and she looked happy with a kerchief around her neck. "We're turning at a place called Mar, and the first one to see the sign gets a nickel."

"I do," Tessa shouted, "right up there."

"Moth—er!" Janie groaned. "You're going to have to turn this kid in to the cops."

"No, Jane, she's right, there it is," said Frank. "We turn left and in about two miles we drive over a causeway over Sky Lake."

"It's a hot day," said Maudie, "and a long drive for you, Frank."

Mar, Mar, Mars, thought Tessa. Mars and Sky take us to Star Bay.

"I see Sky Lake!" Jane shouted, straining through her spectacles. And she did. And it was full of lily pads. And the causeway rumbled as they drove over it.

They had hung over Dr Arnold's map night after night at home, and Tessa, who was put to bed long before Janie, lay sleepless, dreaming of it: up the Peninsula to Mar, to Sky Lake, down a road through the bush to Star Bay. And Dr Arnold had promised them the perfect place, and he would know, because he was special: he was curing her father. He'd even made him stop smoking, and that other time they went away he sent huge bottles of thick pink medicine in wooden boxes with dovetailed ends, lined like chocolate boxes with padding, that would have made good doll beds, only they had to send them back. That was when she was four, and they sat watching the men carve the Presidents on Mount Rushmore, looking like ants on irritated faces (she kept waiting for the noses to twitch).

The Snail Family at Large, she thought. She was already a reader.

After the boggy lake, the road turned south. It was narrow and twisting, and the woods shouldered in at them on either side. Father blew the horn before every little rise and turning: they had a big car and a big trailer, and everyone needed to be warned.

"It looks like nothing," the doctor had warned. "It takes a while to find out it's heaven."

It was the last day of June, and hot, though somewhat cooler as they proceeded through the woods. The road turned from gravel to sand and they had to turn right — "towards the lake," Frank said to Maudie, who never knew where she was. They went through scrubby cedar bush hedged by snake fences, past a tumbledown farm. "That'll be Ellis's, we'd better stop."

"No!" cried Tessa. "I want to get there."

"Shuddup, kid," said Janie, because her parents were already out of the car. She got out too, and Tessa was going to, but when she went to open her door, there was a big sort of duck there staring at her and hissing. The sound was dreadful, dry and angry. The creature had a thick yellow tongue but it didn't stick out, it curved meanly up. It took Tessa a long time to learn to hiss like that.

They found her cowering. "Oh, I know what you mean, Tess," said Maudie. "I always hated geese. And did I tell you about the time my brother Will found me down in the barnyard and the turkey cock was pecking at me?"

"Not exactly friendly," the father said.

"No, but she likes to rule her own roost."

"I thought she was very interesting," said Janie.

"She has a boy about your age," Maudie said.

Janie huffed and puffed.

It was only a little way now: the lake was already there, looking grey because the sun was so bright. There wasn't a road along the beach, they just turned and humped along a track, past two cottages, big ones, and then two little ones, and over a log bridge. "There it'll be," Frank said.

"Oh," said Maudie, because she was looking at nothing. A dump of old cans, a half-fallen chimney. "You can get out, girls," she said.

Janie got out her side, and went into conference at once with the adults. Tessa finally wrangled her door open, found no goose-guardian, and stepped into her world. A stony beach, thin, shallow water with well-spaced grasses growing in it and look — but nobody was there to look, they were parking and levelling and doing whatever they did with the trailer so they could open the door without having it slam right into their faces — look, there are tiny little fish, there. And then there was a big island, and further out, a paradise of little islands. Tessa took off her shoes, and then her socks. She put them neatly down on a rock, tucked her new seersucker shirt into her new seersucker shorts, and set off to find her world.

She didn't have to go far. She just lay down on the sand and began to stare into the water. Very small fish nipped from reed to reed: it was enough.

"Tessa . . . Tess—a."

They had done their things now, even had the two folding chairs and two folding stools in a row facing the beach and parallel to it. "It's your job to get the flowers," her mother said, "and, oh, put on your shoes."

New Sisman Scampers.

What could the flowers have been that June? Because later she remembers cinquefoil and pearly, everlasting fireweed. But they are August flowers. And when do the harebells, leaf-less and blue, come out?

The trailer door faces inland, and when Tessa returns with much-praised flowers the table is already set, Janie has been sent somewhere to get a pail of water, and the naptha gas stove is lit and Maudie is scrambling eggs. Soon enough, they seal the place up against mosquitoes and they're lying in their bunks in the last glow of the Coleman lantern. If Tessa re-members that it was because she couldn't keep her fingers off the rainy tentsides that they got the trailer, she doesn't remind herself. She dreams of touching the glowing, forbidden mantle of the lamp.

Does she hear her mother whisper to her father, "But there's nothing here, Frank, nothing?" If she does, she doesn't care. Janie, who is elderly and responsible, turns heavily in her sleep.

All the years of summer in heaven run together and who can tell how many there were? Two? Three? Five? Janie got big in the summers there, and pretty enough to get the better of her glasses, and modest enough to hide with a flurry that knocked the upper bunk down on Tessa's head the night Joey Ellis came late with the ice. Tessa was never big there, never awkward (though old Mrs Ellis kept saying, "don't send that Tessa for the milk, she's that clumsy she'll fall into the spring"), never fell out of heaven.

Because even her talent for vomiting became an asset; even

the war became her ally: once they got the use of a boat, or whichever boat her father was fixing up for whichever cottage, Tessa was firmly left on shore and for what seemed a wonderful eternity she was in possession of paradise.

They got up early, slipped into their bathing suits, or their seersucker costumes. Mother went out and got their washcloths off the line and they went down to the water to wash their faces. There was drama if the Pike boys from Detroit, whose mother was supposed to be a German spy, had been along first and tied garter snakes to the clothes-line, which was a tow rope. Then Maudie had to decide whether to be merciful and untie the snakes, be sluttish and let the girls go dirty, or go in and fry the eggs. Frank was already off tinkering with something somewhere: how he spent his life.

Then suddenly everyone was gone, there was no one to call her Tillie the Toilet, there was nothing to do and everything to do. No other kids — the Pike boys weren't kids, and they only wanted to get a look at Janie and hand out snakes — no one her age: only Tess and the beach.

She ran and ran and ran. She outran sandpipers and caught their babies, holding the fuzzy balls in her hands before she let them go again, being careful not to hold too tight, because last spring on Uncle Will's farm . . . She outran Popeye, Joey Ellis's black and white dog, and nobody believed her but when she threw a stick in the water for him down further by the big dock where the fishermen's boats were, threw it good and far out into the water, the dog swam after it and his green coating of fleas rose from the water and hovered over him, hopping through the air. Nobody believed her, but it happened.

There was a fair number of cottages, most empty. The two next to them belonged to the Pennypackers from Buffalo. Then there was the Crow's Nest, owned by a man named Crow who never spoke. Past the creek where the live box was, there was Sovereigns' place: they had a niece called Dorothy Crown. Over the road from there was a man called Grimes and even though his cottage was empty Janie and Tessa went mad with embarrassment when their mother sang, in her church contralto, "Old Grimes is dead, that dear old man" as they passed it when they took a stroll in the evening.

But the evenings weren't the best time: the lone mornings were: running alone on the beach, king of the castle on every rock and *no one to see*! No one to say, don't, Tessa.

There was only one rule. It all ends if you swim alone. It was like Uncle Will's farm: it all ends if you try to get on a horse. You can be, but you can't do. A bad rule for later life, it turned out, but she couldn't have known that.

Probably, they could always see her from where they fished. But she did not feel watched.

There was lunch when they got back; then a nap; then swimming. She learned to swim, but so did her mother, the very same day, and scooped her. They all except Janie, who got something prettier from the catalogue, had woollen bathing suits. Her father's had big holes in the sides. Hers took the skin off her thighs: it was pink.

If she stayed too long in the sun she got sick, disgusting them all with her vomiting. Mostly she remembered to keep on her hat.

There was much to see, and when they were swimming she lay in the shallows and felt the minnows nibbling at her with their soft puckering little mouths. One year when the water was low she and Jane swam out to the island, but she got scared when she got turned out to face the open lake and had to be rescued.

The islands out there were called the Fishing Islands and there were certainly a lot of fish. Every night they had bass for supper. Tessa went to the live box with her father and helped to pick them out, big sturdy fellows, all over eight inches because that was the rule. Among them sometimes there were beautiful little baby fish that had hatched in the creek, but it was against the law to take them home and put them in a jar, Frank said.

Then he sat in the grove of cedars by the trailer and filleted the fish with a special knife he had bought in South Dakota for trout. The nasty part came when it was Tessa's job to take the cleanings out on an aluminum plate to the seagulls. She hated it, it was a rock she played King of the Castle on she had to set the plate on, and the gulls were always expecting her and swooped down greedily. Their wings were beautiful and they looked as if they could knock your head off: they were sharp and clean as a shining knife. She never got out of the job. Or failed, later, to eat as many delicious slivers of bass as she could obtain.

She must have grown up: one summer two English children came, and she hated them, and they hated her, and that was that. She collected a whole Campbell's soup can of baby toads and fixed them in the crotch of a cedar tree, to have someone to talk to, but the wind blew it over. Her mother said. Once a week she was allowed to overturn a certain board in the clearing and watch the ants carry their Rice Krispies away. In the evenings they sat in a row outside, listening to the nighthawks boom and cry. They mewed like cats sometimes. A bat took up residence inside the window by Janie's bunk, and they didn't dare open it all summer: they lay and watched him hanging upside down. He had an evil-looking nose, but he was very shy.

When the mosquitoes got bad they went indoors and went through the ritual of watching Father light the Coleman lantern. (Father was the most important person in the world: nobody else could control naptha gas.) Then they played rummy, trying to beat him, but he could remember the cards. Then they went to bed and lay in their beds singing "Redwing" and "When It's Springtime in the Rockies," and (Tessa was patriotic and the war was still on, always on) "There'll Always Be an England." "The White Cliffs of Dover" was too high for Mother.

Tessa got old enough to go up to the spring house for milk, through the woods instead of up the road, because she hated, vividly and personally, the geese, who hated her, surrounded her when she tried to take a step. Once, dreaming, swinging the tin billycan, she walked straight into a cow and ran home so fast that she spilled not a drop, and it took her mother an hour to get a description of the monster.

Janie must have had another life, but sometimes they went somewhere together. Once up to the Big Sand Pile, a strip of dunes inland towards the forest road. There were other children with them, and they threw themselves down the hillocks of fine white sand screaming and crying and rolling as if it were snow: then a rattlesnake slithered across the bottom of a dune, its tail sizzling like dried peas in a gourd and they fell silent and after it went home, they went home.

Other things happened: she took up catching baby leopard frogs for fishermen. One of them paid her in stale humbugs instead of money and her mother taught her about business. Her father made friends with a fat man from Buffalo, a cooper, who admired a mechanical man and invited them to come to his cottage for steak and ice cream from Mrs Ellis's cows, churned in a big vessel with a crank. One of Jane's friends rubbed poison ivy on her face to see what would happen. Tessa made a friend, and then she went away.

How many summers? Who can tell? Tess has tried to ask Jane, Jane has tried to remember: neither of them knows. They lead different lives, and Star Bay wasn't important to Jane: she had no leopard frog business, she had other things on her mind, the time just went.

Once they went into the woods together, the forbidden woods, and Jane was the leader, and Jane, with her mother's gifts, got lost. "We must sit and wait, Tess, until they come and find us," she said piously. "That's what Daddy said."

Tess sat on a log as long as she could, a whole minute. "Look, Jane, the sun sets over the lake and it's afternoon and there's the sun so if we walked we get to the beach, see?"

"Tess, we are to sit and wait until we are rescued. Otherwise we will walk in circles. People die that way."

Tess, conscious as Jane that she was the great-grandchild of pioneers, extended her arm. "Look, Janie, you stick out your arm and at the end of it are your fingers, and you put them between the sun and the horizon: each one is fifteen minutes. It's only about three o'clock.''

''Tess, stay there.''

''Well, you can stay there. I'm going to the beach, and when I get there I'm turning left.'' She skittered off, leaving Janie, scared, in a mossy cathedral of a clearing, trying to decide how best to be elderly and responsible. Reluctantly, she followed Tess.

They came out somewhere they'd never been before and even Tess was scared for a minute, but she knew home was left. She danced ahead and Jane followed sulkily. ''Look,'' she cried finally, ''we're on the other side of the clearing, look!'' Janie, stubborn and humiliated, looked down instead of ahead and saw that the rarest of treasures, a leaf-coloured whippoorwill on her nest. They sat down and worshipped, not daring to breathe. The bird's whiskers twitched, her eyes rolled with fear, she was as quiet as they were. When they got up and tiptoed home she flopped off, but only a little way, for a little while. When they looked back she was back with her eggs. They went home hand in hand and told their adventure.

Then something happened: their father was given a job teaching on an army base. He wouldn't turn it down: his First War service record put him in an excellent category (though he wouldn't join up and be a Captain, once was enough, he said, and civilian staff got better pay); everything about the job was advantageous, especially having a sergeant to handle the discipline. They moved. Janie set out to conquer her eleventh school. Tess was no longer thin and faster than a sandpiper. There were only two weeks' holidays, and Father's ulcers were cured.

They never went back. Frank and Maudie didn't believe in going back anywhere. And anyway, wouldn't Tess like to go to summer camp with the girl next door? They could afford it now. So Tess went to camp and her parents took the green trailer somewhere by themselves. Janie was fruit-picking.

It might even have been thirty years later that Tess and her husband were driving down the Bruce from Tobermory, arguing who had overspent on the holiday. There was a big green sign, "Mar," on the highway, and Tess, who never learned to drive said, "Oh, please." He gave her his Kismet look and sighed. "We can have lunch there." The children were asleep in the back of the car.

She began to bounce. "Sky Lake," she said. The way he looked at it, she knew it was a plain patch of swamp. The road through the bush had been widened, but he honked for her pleasure. The children didn't wake.

At Ellis's, she said, "I'll just get out and get a quart of milk."

He said he'd stay with the kids, but got out of the car and stood against the fender, not unpleased to find himself beside a tumbledown farm in a sandy wilderness.

She asked for a quart of milk in the store, which was a farm kitchen, then confessed, "We used to come in the summer. We had a trailer."

"Oh, you're the Chalmers girl, you write for the papers and you married a Jew. I heard about you. Well, it's not the same place, we sold off a lot of cottage lots. And don't you try to put up your tent or your trailer: we don't allow that now. People aren't what they used to be." She went on for a bit about how they didn't eat what was put before them, either, and how she'd married Joey's brother and taken over the store from the old lady, who died a couple of years ago, she was a hundred.

Tess, conscious of Sam out there waiting, said well, it was nice to see her, and where was the milk?

"Don't you remember? Why, it's out where it's always been, in the spring house, by the road. And don't fall in." Then she told her how her husband had had a foot cut off because of the diabetes and the other one would soon have to go, which was pity because for a while he was Township Reeve.

Tess felt guilty going down the path, as if, like Elmer Ellis, she'd eaten too many chocolate bars. Sam was still by the car, but she couldn't quite remember where the springhouse was, and she was tense: then she thought, it's the geese and the old woman, I was scared of the geese and the old woman.

Right at the bottom of the path, where the wire fence with pressed iron maple leaves between its scallops left off, there was a wooden shed. It was open to the road, so she had only one gate to go through. She walked in: it was new inside, all concrete, but there was a funny smell. There was a concrete floor, and it had certainly been earth before, and there were wire baskets containing waxed-paper cartons of milk, not billycans or bottles or whatever there were before, and she half closed her eyes and reached forward.

Then she remembered: because around each carton there was a garter snake coiled. And the smell was sulphur because it was a sulphur spring. She took her milk and half ran to the car.

"Home?" Sam laughed.

"Sort of. Oh, look, two rows of cottages, like a subdivision. That was the Little Sand Pile. It was always full of cow pies."

"Glamorous." He wasn't particularly urban, but he had gone to more expensive camps: he expected his wilderness to be up to a certain standard.

They got down to the lake. There was a new dock, but not a very good one. The ice house had collapsed. Sovereigns' and Grimes' and Crows' cottages were exactly as they had been before. "That's Sunset Island," she said, pointing at it. It looked terrible: a mud blob in a mercury pool. The day was so hot everything had flattened out.

She got out the food box and set about making some sandwiches. The children woke up and were so overheated she set them down in their shorts in the shallow water. Nobody wanted any milk. The children paddled in the water and pronounced it yucky. Sam told her to go for a walk: he would baby-sit.

She set out. Mrs Ellis had told her the Blue Cottage was for sale. She went past it and Pennypackers' and came to their own clearing: it was exactly the same. The cedar grove was still the shape of a woodshed or a living-room. She might find the aluminum plate for the fish cleanings if her parents had been the sort of people who ever left an object behind. But they had littered with memories, and she had become the sort of person who picked them up after them. And if she went looking for the board with the ants under it, or the can of toads, or the scars of the tow-rope against the tree, or the whippoorwill's nest, what wouldn't happen. Anyway, she was too big to be king of the castle any more. She heard her mother's voice, "You won't remember, but that first day up there, I thought, what's happening to us now, what is this place, how can we bear it?"

She turned back towards Sam and the children and saw in the distance because she was still long-sighted a tall athletic woman walking, and remembered a certain woman, another non-Canadian, a minister's daughter from California who used to organize games on the beach. She pelted back to Sam. "Let's pack up. There's someone coming."

Ten years after that, she thought, would it have helped if I had said something artistic like "Od und leer das Meer?" And laughed, and plunged her hand in again among the cold bottles and the cold snakes and smelled sulphur.

In the Sun

In the Sun

Because she is early, she comes up from the subway a stop ahead of her destination; when she is on street level, in the light, she blinks in confusion at the Medical Arts Building, wondering which appointment she has. Is it the dentist, the gynaecologist? Something — perhaps the trauma of passion through the gate that is so much like an iron maiden that it frightens her every time — has made her forget where she is going. She pushes at the PULL door, gets it right, goes into the sunshine, and, as she is about to step out to cross the road, remembers. This is no dentist's appointment; she is wearing her good dress and high heels and lipstick. This is the day she is having lunch with that lovely man.

I'm old, she thinks, and before my time.

Preoccupied, rather; still, it shakes her when this happens. And she is in an odd mood today, something to do with her dreams perhaps, an unremembered confusion of scrambles and loops, some statement of victory before waking early to the cry of the baby next door and the nuzzling of the cat. One moment I'm out to lunch, she thinks, now I'm going to lunch.

She walks down to Bloor Street without turning her ankle

on the rough paving, always a good sign, and manages to turn the corner without bumping into anyone. The day is brisk and sunny, cooler than yesterday, exactly to her taste. Not many days a year here when it is neither too hot nor too cold, when the air is like silk on the skin and one dreams of the pleasures of the flesh.

Oh, Sylvie, she mutters to herself, is that where you are, and at your age?

Why not, her other self says: Justinian Lewis is a handsome man. She looks at her watch again. Still early.

She grew up puritan, she is always embarrassed by the enthusiasm of her sexuality, but at least it no longer surprises her. Justinian Lewis, who is over from England to produce a television program on a subject that is her specialty, is tall, well tailored and well spoken. His invitation is flattering, and she likes the hotel he is taking her to.

But something else is happening to her in these split moments in the sunshine, something that happens frequently now, that is akin to forgetting but is a kind of remembering, and it appals her. Perhaps this is what it feels like to be an insect or a reptile that splits its skin: a cicada launching itself into a new life by shedding the old carapace, though that discarded shell could hardly be a carapace if a carapace was an external skeleton; she must look it up. But she was consciously in the sun here beside the red brick wall which last, last spring was carefully mended, as the wall of her house should have been, splitting and shedding. And what she is shedding is the adult part of her consciousness; it is peeling away from her, leaving her vulnerable, soft-shelled. She cannot go on. She is barely able to walk. She is Little Sylvie, the baby, the straggler, the one who could not or would not keep up, the one who hopped on one foot in concentric patterns while the others stood and talked, deciding endlessly who would go in whose car.

The little one, dumb one, stumblebum, leafhopper; the one who ran from one end of the house to the other trying to split her body against the fine force of the walls: look at Sylvie, Mum, look at what that stupid kid is doing now.

The little one. The one with the Ph.D.

Oh, there is joy in it: to see oneself in a plate-glass window, stout and middle-aged in a good dress and good shoes, to know that one is wearing little white socks and buckle shoes and hopping; much more interesting to travel on one foot and watch the faces on one's shoes; lovely to be garbed so simply, in a dress and a pair of pants, socks, shoes: air at the armpits and the world above gay and green. Friends with the birds and the wandering, scurrying squirrels. I am four, she thinks. Then, passing a window, seeing two wings of white in her brown hair; three, perhaps.

She is still early. There is time to harden the new body in the sun. She sits carefully in order not to soil the dress, pull its threads on the rough concrete, on the edge of a square planter big enough to hold a sycamore tree. Around the roots of the tree the city has planted a mass of heliotrope of the variety ridiculously (considering that heliotrope is usually heliotrope coloured) called Cherry Pie. The child inside her shrieks, "Can you make a cherry pie?" high and off tune. She lights a cigarette.

Woman with grey middle-aged silk bottom sits hatching outside Royal Bank surrounded by heliotrope. It is growing into her lap and she is remembering arguments about what was heliotrope, what was magenta, what was bougainvillaea: the things they fought about in their house over the set of Eagle Prismacolour Pencils, Fred's books of drafting paper on which each pencil made a variation of its colour according to the texture of the paper. Ellen drawing hats. All of them on wet Sundays busy at the dining-room table. "Mum, Sylvie's chewing pencils again!"

There's still time. She moves away from the planter, retracing her footsteps, a thing she has never liked to do but now finds practical, to take a place on the bench in the walled garden beside the Institute for Studies in Education where a friend of hers designs feminist board games. I have to grow up, she thinks, I have to grow her up. In fifteen minutes.

She takes the child like a pea out of a pod, catches her before she flies off like milkweed floss (was it rubber or parachute silk people meant to make out of the milkweed pods they gathered during the war?) and sets her firmly on the bench beside her. She's a bonnie child in her white dress and shoes and socks, a pink Kitty Higgins bow in her cornsilk hair. "Sit still," she says firmly, beginning to smooth and tend her.

Four, five, six, seven. She sits there, watching the child growing.

Why now? Why with Justinian Lewis? Slipping a cog, slipping so many that the chain unreels that far backwards?

A tall man, broad in the chest; curly hair, white sideburns; good profile, friendly smile. Not one who dismisses women her age.

What is this about?

Oh, criminy: Daddy.

Sylvie in a white dress, being an airplane, careening towards Daddy and sexual mistakes. Sylvie, tendrils sprouting from her fingers, curling around Daddy like a succubus. Sylvie grown up, surprised to find that Daddy is a small man.

She picks the child up tenderly, soothes and smoothes her again, retying the bow, wiping a spot of soot from her nose with a tissue, tickling her a little, patting her. "If you'll only grow up," she whispers, "not all the way, just a little, I'll — I'll, why I'll buy you a stick of red licorice."

Then she sets the child on her feet, gets off the bench, straightens her dress, takes the child's hand and begins to walk east towards the hotel.

I'll have the sole, she thinks; it will be easier for a young person to manage.

Banana Flies

Banana Flies

Now I want to flap my arms and fly. Something's happening: I am a bird in the shape of a banana peel, going far, but not to the terminus.

Let's play games. Let me tell you a true story and pretend it's unreal. Let me tell you an unreal story and you make it real.

The true story is that we had a dinner party and nothing happened except that skeletons were made of birds. But something did happen: I came home happy and I didn't mind the banana peel on the coffee-table. I am still happy. Something happened.

To make it fiction we have to change the names. I sat beside Almond and across from Pear. I am Apple, because I've always wanted to be Eve. I'm not, but because it is I who push the keys of the typewriter, I can choose to be.

The party was given by Cherry in honour of Almond, who was supposed to be leaving for Figland. In fact she is not: she is having an affair with Lime Rickey and not upset by the cancellation of her voyage, although she needs a new job.

I have left out Greengage, because I do not know her well.

Mirabelle, whom you may prefer to call Victoria Plum, was next to Cherry. She is the only one of us who is still married. I don't see enough of her. She made a wicked birthday punch in baby-days.

It was happy, that evening. We were in full fig. Nothing has been changed but the names.

These are the facts: we talked and talked. Pear talked of her travels. I talked of my desire to travel. Everyone talked about going south to visit Pear on her island; how to rival Pear in parsimony. She is the cleverest of us all, the high-wire dancer among us acrobats. The oldest, too, an empty-nester, while most of us are just beginning to wave goodbye. Almond's boys left this year, Apple is between hope that they will and despair that they might, Mirabelle doesn't know how she feels, Cherry cherishes her five-year-old, dreaming dreams we have outgrown. Greengage moved out, leaving the Independence Party behind, and bought new furniture.

It was Pear who dominated, Pear who all her life had done more with less, and has taught us much: live, fill up the cup, be the cup, shed your leaves when the time comes.

"What movie star did you want to be?"

"Hedy Lamarr," she said.

I confessed to lacquered Merle Oberon, whom my mother-in-law humanized by using the surname Obrien. Long-legged singers and dancers came in, and small blonde flesh-pots. We sighed for our stupidity, and laughed at the greasy lovers we had desired. What movie star did you want to sleep with, before you dared to think what that meant?

The past, the future, hope. Pear's first divorce told with exquisite humour: a bunch of pulp magazine writers concocting a story too good for the judge, mission accomplished with bated breath.

Almond's pride in her boys.

Mirabelle's happiness: to have survived a most difficult marriage, to have fine children. She is kind and tolerant.

So are we all, this group of women under the lamplight, the anthropological decorations from other days.

It was the sort of party men might have called, in my day, a hen party. It wasn't a stag.

We ate two birds and a garden of vegetables, grapes and cheese and a pineapple cut to look like a pheasant. The Brie abandoned itself. Cherry provided.

Cherry and Almond passed a joint. Pear refused most intoxicants. Apple was at the grape.

There was not a lemon among us.

The divorces, the struggles, the love of children, of irresponsible men, the leaving or staying: the desire for the new. Resignation, hope, search for new places. Give us the country, I wanted to say, we outgrew the movie stars, moved into reality, did it. O'erleapt mothers' neuroses, grandmothers' proprieties, fears, madnesses, the strictures of the men in our lives, judges, doctors, mountebanks. Became.

This group of women around this table, who had met misfortune, alienation, fame, success, disgrace, competence, love, hate, disaster, disorientation, fear, the love of children. Learned to raise them, learned to part with them and move on.

Apple to Pear: I became an "art" writer because I was supported by Potato.

Pear to Apple: He was more of a salmon and you're allergic to fish.

Sense of accomplishment: I am the winged supermarket basket I saw in the performance at the art gallery. The banana, too, the banana I found on the coffee-table crouched like a spread spider which instead of annoying me grew wings.

Have you ever noticed a banana peel flying, how its wings flip and soar, five segments in the sky soaring to the garbage can with elegance and eloquence? All fear of loneliness, falling objects, obscenity, falls away.

Apple speaking. Dinner party over. Send flowers to Cherry. Go to bed. Cover yourself up: you are your own child.

Could I Have Found a Better Love Than You?

NOTES ON THE LIFE OF MISS IRIS
TERRYBERRY WITH EXCERPTS FROM THE
TERRYBERRY GARDEN PERENNIAL CATALOGUE

Could I Have Found
a Better Love Than You?

NOTES ON THE LIFE OF MISS IRIS
TERRYBERRY WITH EXCERPTS FROM THE
TERRYBERRY GARDEN PERENNIAL CATALOGUE

I was tired that evening, tired to the point of being moth-eaten and frail. Ben caught me dozing in the living-room. "You've been out there again," he said. "Why do you do it?"

"One, I'm a nationalist, two, I'm a Terryberry-watcher, three, I'm the Cancer Society Lady, four, I'm meals-on-wheels, five, she's my friend."

"Would you fall over if you had a drink with me?"

"Check the oven when you're in the kitchen, will you?"

When the children were half-way through high school I wanted to go back into the work-force with the rest of my generation, but Ben was against it. "Not on principle," he said, "but because I'm a selfish bastard." I would have fought him on the principle, but the selfishness got to me. Ben and I have a lot in common that way. And there aren't many jobs in Indigo. And I hated teaching when I was single.

So I busied myself in the way of middle-aged women, doing good works and visiting the sick, collecting material for

county archives: living the life of Ladies in Hats, a life for
which I had had contempt when I was young. We didn't need
a second income, but I needed more contact with other minds,
other sets of feelings and experiences. I don't know how my
mother and her friends endured their captivity. The drink
Ben poured me was a stiff one. ''You always sound jealous of
Iris,'' I said. The weak spring sun slanted through the
window-panes and lit up the last of the forced hyacinths on the
coffee-table. They suddenly exhaled a waft of perfume and
the place smelled like a funeral parlour.

''You come home tired from her.''

''Do you know what we did today?''

''You look as if you turned out the attic.''

''We sat out in the forecourt and went through the button
box. She had a bunch of those weights they used to put in
women's skirts to keep them from blowing around. I'd forgot-
ten.'' I like Ben because he's genuinely gregarious, he likes
people and is interested in everything about them.

''And then you cleaned the kitchen sink, emptied the
chamber pot, scalded the pots and pans, and made tea.''

''Well, that. And when I emptied the chamber pot, she
piped up, 'A centipede a pint and a millepede a quart'; my bit
of folklore for the day. I must put it in the notebook.'' I got up
and kissed him on his rising forehead. ''I'd have sat in the sun
with you, Ben, if you were there to sit with.'' In the voice I
used to use for Little Ben.

Ben doesn't sit in the sun: he likes running around and
doing all those things you do in the good rich middle part of
your life when you know a lot and still have energy, like making fast deals and playing fast squash. He's not ready to sit
back and admire life yet. I passed into that category when I
was ill last year.

Perhaps, however, it is not so much ageing and weakness
that make me able to sit quietly with her, walled away from
the elements in the little square between house, greenhouse,
and drive shed, in the ell between the blue potting sheds and
the lily-field, shaded by elm and esker. I was a dreamy, quiet
child and I love my life when it's sluggish as a fat, green river.

Mrs Boronski does the cleaning, Palmer's delivers the groceries, Ben makes his own breakfast: I have time for Iris.

And I've been a Terryberry-watcher for a long time. My mother was one before me, and the whole community has been from time to time. They've never been quite like other people. They've always been first off to wars and gold-rushes, taking up land in the west or California life-styles long before the rest of us. They're bell-wethers, or opportunists, depending on how you think. The first divorced man in Indigo was Dennis Terryberry, the dentist; Tossie was our first OBE, for nursing in World War I; the judge was always a man to watch in his white summer suit, ribboned pince-nez and a rose-bud in his lapel as if it were the Legion of Honour. Dr Carscadden is thinking of declaring Ronnie our first case of confirmed Alzheimer's disease — though he appears to have had it most of his life — and then there's Iris.

I didn't grow up in Indigo, but Mother was from here and I knew the town from visits to innumerable farm relatives on the periphery and trips (in the buggy during the war: how we loved them!) to the Co-op and the creamery. When Ben and I moved here, the first Terryberry I met was Mrs Wilt Terryberry, the undertaker's wife, an abrasive woman if ever there was one. I remember asking her for a division of a particularly lovely peony she had. "Buy your own," she snarled. I was so hurt I didn't mention it to anyone for months. Then I told Mary Gaskin, who said, "Oh, but she wanted you to go to Iris." When I said, "Who's Iris?", another part of my life began.

Terryberry's Favourite: Rich mauve standards, flamboyant violet falls, heavily ruffled and gartered in purple. Try a cluster of chorus girls at your door. Mid-season, $4 and worth it.

I went to university because Mother had wanted to go. She was like that, felt I should live the life she had failed to have. She said I shouldn't cry because Bill Fairchild married someone else, careers were the thing for women now, teaching, that would sustain me. It wasn't pearls before swine for me, it

was decaying mangels to scrawny chickens. Then Mother
summoned me back to London because she was ill, and for
something to get me out of the house I took up giving English
lessons to newly-arrived immigrants. Ben was new to the
country but never young. He was fascinated by the beauty
and availability of old brick farmhouses in the area, talked me
into buying the old Elder place. Mother thought it a poor investment, and as for my marrying a poor ''Bohemian'' immi-
grant (we used a word she might like if not understand) who
sold insurance to farmers — Ben thought she was funny and
tugged me away from her to a life of rescuing old houses and
raising children.

And since houses and children go with flowers, I started to
make gardens, filling them with peonies with the lushness of
nursing mothers, scarlet military poppies, starry-eyed phlox
and trusses of daylilies and iris, which I eventually started to
buy from Miss Terryberry, ''The one who never married.''

At first I couldn't find the place, expecting sun glinting on
greenhouses in a wide field. Iris's establishment was screened
from the road by a clump of cedar and built into the side of the
north-facing ridge of gravel that gives this countryside its
character, the Long Esker. Her house was a vague arrangement of shanties and chimney-pots she had brought from
another site and attached to one wing of the glasshouses in
order to save on heat. The arrangment looked scatty and run-
down the day I first went there, looking among stacks of
bagged fertilizer, stray kittens, and brown dogs for a sign that
said ''Office'' and finding none. ''We aren't what we were,''
she said when I found her, ''but maybe I have something you
want.''

*Judge's Fancy: Full-headed, showy magenta double peony that visibly
struts in the field. Mid-season, long-lasting. Isolate this colour from the
others and its appeal will double.*

It makes me boil with anger when people say Canadians
have no history. When I was a child I wondered if I would ever

escape the tales of ingrown passion and petty quarrels the matrix of Scots-Irish and English in the county bred. One got tired of wagons breaking down at the right fence corner, horses pausing before sleeping babies in fields, wrong-headed marriages and elopements to Chicago, diphtheria deaths (always the pretty daughter: the plain one pulled through), losses to foreign wars. I was one of the generation which tried for a while to cover that porous historical brick and wood with the hard tile of sophistication, dropping the last of the forced handicrafts, feeding on the new and glittering values imported from postwar Europe; but I too returned to the matrix and raised children and found I needed after all grey churches, things hanging from rafters, bleeding-heart.

Terry's Favourite: Rich mauve standards, violet falls, heavily ruffled, veined purple, rosy stamens, tall, a sensation, $5.95 and worth every penny.

She didn't talk much at first, but there were things I wanted that opened her up to me: monkshood, cottage pinks. She was famous far beyond the boundaries of the county for her old flowers, iris, daylily, peonies, single roses.

''The judge got us all around the dining-room table when I was maybe eight or nine and read us the riot act about making something of ourselves, even the girls,'' she said. ''There was nothing worse than greed without ambition, he said, and there was a lot of it in this house — Mother was a wonderful cook and there seemed to be barrels of sugar cookies in the kitchen — and in general he fired us up. George went into law, Dennis figured the county needed a dentist, and he'd have done all right if he hadn't taken up with poor Lily Mills, no brain and no health, though she was a pretty, pale thing — and Tossie went for nursing. He wanted me to train for a teacher but I didn't like the idea any more than you liked the fact, and I always liked the garden. He'd have let me stay home if I was any good around the house, but I was clumsy and dreamy, so he got me work as a trainee with a breeder he knew in Holland, Michigan. Mother might have objected to my going away so soon: I was only sixteen — but she was completely taken up with Ronnie by then, and Wilf was off somewhere learning to be an undertaker.

"He was a fair man, the judge, and well-liked, though I didn't like him. Whatever you said, he had to go one better. When I was about 15, I remember your mother's brother Will came calling on a Sunday afternoon, and I liked him; but we were playing some kind of parlour game and he said he wasn't going in with any cutthroat Terryberrys, and that was that.

"Father fought me all the way. When he saw me working in greenhouses, he decided it wasn't a good job for a lady. This piece of land was known as Uncle Beau's Bog before I bought it with my savings. I camped out here in a tent the first summer. Father fussed and fumed and I let him. First he bought me a dog, then he helped me set up the cottage: just a bare shelter, one of the drive-sheds from behind Wilt's. He said the whole enterprise was bad for his reputation. I didn't care. I'd never had a come-hither eye. There's no glamour in men to a girl with four brothers.

"I didn't give a darn about my personal life, I put everything I had into getting the business going. I wanted to show him I could do something. In the twenties this was a good go-ahead business, and in the thirties it was famous, though the problem was always the same: when times were good, you couldn't get help, and when there was help, nobody had any money for flowers. I specialized in spring perennials because if you've got the patience for them, the return is good. Of course then we sold a lot of shrubs and bush fruit and the usual box plants: styles change but petunias and marigolds are the things that do well.

"He was an old tyrant, Father. When he was dying I went into Indigo every night to sit with him. He'd worry away at me, 'Iris, Iris, you never married.' I used to think, 'Men are weak creatures, they have to be placated with pie. I'd get elected prime minister, he'd never notice.' That was the year

I took medals at four exhibitions here and two in Michigan. I was just an old maid to him.''

Terry's Treasure: 28'' daylily, early, a miracle: velvet petals a heavily ruffled apricot; green throat circled pale gold. Rich, meaty clusters, well-branched and graceful. Colour holds all day, a prize-winner.

''Now here are the old catalogues. We couldn't afford colour printing, but Wilt's daughter Jessie did me a few little drawings like that phlox. Mr Jackson set it up every year for me in the fall, when I knew what was going to be ready for spring. I started out very scientific, but I discovered that what people want isn't science, it's novelty, a blue version of a yellow flower or a bigger one, or a night flower that stays open all day: something their neighborhood doesn't have already.

''Still, you don't want to go too far with fashion. The nights are long out here, and the flowers don't talk much, so I used to read a lot, philosophy, even, and I remember somebody saying something about all things tending to something — well, in the nursery world, I'll tell you, all things tend to puce. When you see in a catalogue some kind of brown sliding into purple with a green sort of sheen, you know some beggar's made a mistake and he's trying to pass it off. You keep your yellows and your purples segregated and you get back to Eden where colours ran true.''

Ben's insecurities start leaking out when I pay too much attention to anyone else, so I didn't see as much as I wanted to of Iris, but after she broke her hip, when I was with her and counted the number of painful motions she went through even to boil an egg for herself, I started taking her out the meals-on-wheels for dinner, and little lunches of the kind the children and I always loved: a slice of Granny Smith apple cut like a wheel, a crunch of Cheddar cheese, a few wheat crackers and a spoonful of cherry jam, with a thermos of good coffee. We'd sit in the sunlight like children in a nursery and eat, and then

I'd check on her exercises. The doctor was dubious about the hip operation, thought that at her age she might as well take to her bed, but Wilt's nephew Brian Stewart is resident in orthopaedics at one of the big hospitals in London and he got his boss, who is world famous, to insert a prosthesis. They had her up the next day and hobbling on canes in a week, but efficient movement was still a long way off, that day.

"Dr Carscadden's a fine man," she said, "but I don't think he's fond of me. A lot of people aren't. They think I'm a crazy old witch, they think there was something between Ardeen and me, they think I should go into the Home with Ronnie.

"Ronnie was always the funny one. Mother took a look at him the minute he was born and said, 'That one's mine, I'll keep him,' and let him stay a child forever. Ever notice women with big families doing that, keeping the smallest boy for a priest, the one who won't be unfaithful to her?

"Father wasn't much help. He'd be away three months on the circuit and come back grumpy and formal. The tone of the house would change completely. He scared the living daylights out of us: he'd yell at Mother, 'What, no applesauce for tea, what do you mean, woman?' and she'd throw her apron over her face and cry. Tossie said it was a game, but Ronnie and I thought he scared her as much as he scared us. At least I got out in time. Still, he's all right in the Home, Ronnie, he's been senile all his life, his first and second childhoods all mixed up.

"Carscadden was hard on me about Ardeen. He thought I overworked her, but she was one of those terriers, worked all night and all day as if the devil was after her. I didn't know she had a bad heart. She'd had a hard upbringing, all that stuff about the devil finding work for idle hands to do. You know what that's about. What I say is, if the good Lord meant us not to play with ourselves, what was he doing making our arms just the right length?

"I loved Ardeen, I guess, but not in a physical way. There must have been something missing in me, the sex urge didn't come out, or maybe I didn't let myself feel it. Oh, there was a man in Michigan when I was young: a tall, fair, quiet chap with a limp — ever notice how young girls are wild for a man with a limp? — and we'd stand there playing with anthers and stamens and pistils and kind of lean towards each other, but he never said anything, and when you work twelve hours a day, you don't have much energy.''

Ardeen: A clear blue beauty, silver shimmers in the graceful falls, silver-spangled beard. Perfect form, good substance, the grand duchess of irises. Where else can you purchase charm and dignity?

''She just walked in off the road one day and stood by my elbow and after about half an hour said, 'Can I have a job Miss Terryberry?' I was hard up then, I'd have taken a one-legged leper, there was work for twenty. I needed a bunch of POWs like the ones I had in the war, instead I was making do with a couple of hired hands. Carscadden says I worked her to death, but she was one of those driven people, and she'd been raped by the field hands working for a man outside Leamington; she was trying to get it out of her mind. She asked where the bunkhouse was but I put her in the spare room.

''There was all that fuss when Freud said everything was sex; in this part of the world people certainly think it is. They don't want to admit their own feelings so they accuse everyone else of it. They used to say right out Ardeen and I were a pair of lezzies. She was a poor sad thing, and I'd hear her sobbing in the night and go in and make her drink strawberry tea and a couple of times I put my arms around her to comfort her, but I wanted company, not sex, and she never offered me any. She followed me like a shadow, and I'm human: I lapped up her dumb devotion.

''Those were good years. It isn't complicated work. You have to be orderly and keep good records, marking what you crossed with A or B, and what you bred on itself and what you let the bees do. The big perennials take a long time to make a show, but you can propagate the roots and get them to run true. The return isn't great in this country, we don't have American megalomania or British estates, but there's a small steady market for good stock. The climate doesn't let us go any farther: when there's only five months of decent weather, naturally you think cucumbers instead of rhododendrons. We did all right, and I wasn't a man with a wife to keep in diamonds and furs. Ardeen never asked for anything. When she got shabby I'd take her up to London and dress her as if she was my child.

"She couldn't talk in front of strangers except to say yes, no, it likes a bit of lime, but she was bright around the house in the evening when we had time to talk. She helped me clean out the library. She liked science fiction. She worked on prim-roses for a while, she called them her space flowers, but they don't do well here. She fancied Japanese things, too, and she did a bit of Japanese gardening, training chrysanthemums to fancy patterns and making bonsai trees, but she did better under orders than working on her own. She might have got better if she'd lived.

"The mistake I made was thinking she was thin because she was like me, one of the earth's stringy beasts. She'd get awful coughs and I'd doctor her with garlic soup, whatever was lying around. Neither of us ate much. Then one winter I made her go to Jack Carscadden and it was lungs. He was so mad at me! Cooping her up in a greenhouse he said was the last thing I should have done with her.

"I was afraid they'd take her away from me and put her in the san, but they don't do that any more. The antibiotics fixed her up, but by that time she was weak in the heart. I got this sort of courtyard arrangement fixed up so she could sit in the sun when there was any, but she died that winter. She wouldn't tell anyone who her parents were, so I was registered as her next of kin. She never got any mail when she was here, not so much as a postcard, and there are a lot of Bakers in the world, though not many Ardeens. I felt she might be a Maritimer from her accent, but nobody answered

my ad in the Halifax paper. There aren't many people who
come and go like the wind, but a few do.''

*Major General: Narrow, erect, royal blue standards, lighter blue falls
netted and veined royal; button-brass beard. Stiff, dignified, gleams in
the sun, good against roses.*

I was tired when I got home that night, and the next day
Nancy Fairbanks went out to see Iris, so I stayed home to
prepare for the Historical Society meeting. We had a turnout
of forty-five to hear a woman from Toronto recite verses and
songs from Alice Kane's book about her Ulster childhood,
and it was well after midnight, and raining, by the time they
were able to leave off their reminiscences — one song inevitably produced another and to judge from the way we all knew
them, we were all from Bally-somewhere — and go home. I
woke tired the next day and Ben said he hadn't much to do,
why didn't I stay in bed that day, he would call on Iris, and to
tell the truth I was grateful.

Rest did its magic, however, and by five I had a good dinner on and was watching for him from the window. There was
no sign of him until much later, and I was reading in the study
when the car drove in. He came in the side door without calling out, and I heard him rummaging for ice and glasses at
once, a bad sign. Then the kitchen drawers opening and shutting; he was looking for something. He came towards me
limping, mud on his trousers, a scowl on his face. "For God's
sake, where's the garlic, I've found the string not the garlic.''

"Under the onions.''

He handed me the drinks and went back, returned knotting
a necklace of string and garlic around his neck. "Whatever
happened, Ben?''

"Well, I went out and found her. She's all right. Mud in
your eye!''

"Mud on you.''

"Serves me right for visiting a bastard. She's a witch.''

"Sit down and tell me about it."

"Okay." But first he got himself a second drink.

"Well, I got out there about three, and first I got stuck in the lane. Then when I went to the door there wasn't any answer, and just as I was going to the side to see if I could get through a window in case she was dead on the floor, there was a scurrying and this — creature — came to the door: it had short red hair in a brush cut and wore a long dress striped like a bumblebee. Have you heard of someone called Cordell Wainwright?"

"Oh, Ben, you and Della in the same house!" It made me giggle.

"Well, we were, and it was something. I don't care how famous the guy is, he's weird."

"You didn't come to Canada to turn into a redneck. What was he up to?"

"He had a big portfolio of flower drawings he was doing for her and then he did a sort of dance for me, at her insistence, about being a bumblebee: I think they were laughing at me."

"Probably. Iris gets silly when she's with him. He's a wonderful designer, though."

"You couldn't say the drawings were bad, they were a world, they drew me in, they scared hell out of me. I mean at first they just looked like flowers and then I realized they were, well — perverse."

"He has a way of making things look fleshy and overblown."

"She gave me a cup of tea to revive me and then asked me to go out to the greenhouse and dig peonies for Della; he wasn't very strong, poor thing. At least she gave me some rubber boots."

"Ben, if she's giving Della her peonies, she thinks she's going to die."

Because she had decided not to sell the place and instead of closing up entirely she had closed her enterprise up bit by bit, as if she were a lizard shedding pieces of her tail, now only the very front of the greenhouse was operative, a wide space with

a few favourite plants which could be watered by a spray
system connected to her kitchen tap on days when she was
bedridden. These included two blue tree peonies, treasures
presented years ago by a grower who went to China for them,
which Della had been trying to extract from her for years.
Although she was fond of him — she called him "my dragon-
fly" — she had rapped his knuckles for hinting and called him
a bad boy. "When I'm dead," she always said.

*Della Robbia: Gorgeous pale pink, green at the heart, shading to violet
at petals' edge. White veins and stamens, green anthers. Loose, floating
form, luxuriant bloom, exotic for a Canadian hererocallis.*

On Saturday she seemed very feeble, but she was funny
about Ben. "You should have seen him staring at Della," she
chuckled. "And Della was in one of his moods, I couldn't sup-
press him."

"You didn't want to," I said severely. "You're proud of
Della's eccentricities, if that's what you call them."

"Well, when you consider what he came from, and that
Dennis must be rolling in his grave."

Cordell was the strange fruit of Dennis's eldest son Oliver,
who had raised him on dirt farms and in men's hostels until
the rest of the Terryberrys had taken a hand to rescue him and
send him to a strict Anglican boarding school which taught
mostly Latin and canoeing. "I'm worried; you gave him your
peonies."

"You're jealous."

"You know I've no hand for tree peonies. You said he
couldn't have them until you died."

"He's designing for a textile competition, he'll need
them."

"I'm glad you've a reason. Do that exercise once more. I
can't feel the muscle." I had slid my hand under a buttock
that was mere skin and bone; she pulled knee and butt, but
the muscle had no strength. "You'll have to try harder,
darling."

"You could let an old woman off."

"Have a rest now, while I bring you your tea. If you get just a little strength there your balance will improve."

"It's not balance I need, it's balast." The more she ate, the thinner she got, now.

"You don't look so good yourself," she said. "That Ben wears you out."

I smiled because on the Friday night he had, a little, in a pleasant way. "You wore him out, Iris. He was scared of Della."

"Those dratted he-men are sure it's catching."

"Well, Della's a slap in the face for them. He was impressed by the drawings."

"He's going into dark territory, that boy." I had a vision of Della at the mouth of Hades, blue torch of peony in his hand. Was it joy or terror on his face? "Let's try the exercise again, Iris."

The Herbaceous Peony Cerebrus: A deep maroon with golden stamens, shaggy and rich in form, was perhaps Miss Terryberry's most luxurious contribution to the Canadian garden, though the Terry series of iris cannot be faulted for purity of colour and richness of bloom, and she had a pleasant taste in daylilies. Her output was small — she refused to expand although there were several opportunities — and the select varieties she chose to work with responded almost lovingly to her touch. Whether you went to her for luscious Ellen Terry peonies, Terrylime and -lemon iris, or a basket of pansies and pinks, you felt privileged to be a customer. The old order changeth, there will not be another like her.

CANADIAN PLANT BREEDERS' JOURNAL.

I was late getting out there the morning of her 90th birthday. Ronnie had made a fuss about getting into the car, and the coffee urn wasn't ready when I was passing the church to pick it up. She was sitting up in bed, neatly combed, wearing a pink silk jacket printed with mauve flowers that Della had sent her. She had died in her sleep. Ben came out with the doctor and Wilt's grandson Neil. They took both her and Ronnie away, and I stayed behind to wander the greenhouses and collect odd plants for the guests as she had wanted me to. When Ben came back he dug up a row of firefly lilies she had promised me and that was that.

Or almost that. On the morning of the funeral I had an appointment with Dr Carscadden and asked him sharply what he had really thought of Iris. "Oh, I liked her," he said. "The one I had trouble with was Ardeen. She had the worst case of VD I'd ever seen, and I had a hard time coming to terms with that. I always do."

The funeral was God's own gift to Terryberry-watchers; the whole tribe led by Wilton (now 94 and victorious as the Oldest Surviving T) and Ronnie, who walked with downcast gaze, remote as an alcoholic from what was really going on, but sharp, I thought, in his child's way. Thence down through the generations to children with dark, sharp eyes and mischievous grins, and Della smart in a brass, buttoned blazer. Every florist in Western Ontario sent a wreath.

There was trouble afterwards when Wilton found out that Iris had sold her land to Ben years ago; he made a number of nasty remarks about Jews until Ben's lawyer pointed out that the amount of money that had changed hands was unnecessarily large.

Our wandering Aaron came home from British Columbia and lived out there for a while with his friend Blakey. Aaron hated the work, but Blakey took to it: he has green fingers. When I miss Iris, I go out there and help the boy. It's superbly boring work, but Blakey says, when he starts breeding I may name the flowers.

Louisa's Favourite: A lean brown daylily, meagre-blooming, unruffled, but with golden stamens and strange, silver veins. Dignified, but merry in the breeze; unpredictable: not like anything else you have ever seen.

Share and Share Alike

Share and Share Alike

Happiness is a fragile thing, and alcohol, as I know from the house I grew up in, is dangerous to it. When, therefore, I started to drop in to the bar across the road from the office after work and drink with Max Brady, who was a good court reporter because he knew the system from the inside, I decided that there was something wrong with my life and I'd better fix it up quickly or I'd go the way of my rambunctious Aunt Edith and my father.

So I went home and confronted Jean-Louis; after a marathon talk, we agreed that we had married to spite our mothers and we could not now stand each other; that Caroline was a good kid who didn't deserve parents who went in for silent or boozy wars, and that I could have the use of our barn of a house until she was eighteen. He cleared his studio out of the top floor so I could rent it for enough to pay the taxes. It was a fairly amicable parting, though I admit I put away quite a lot of Scotch when Jean-Louis found a new woman to annoy his mother with almost immediately.

I was putting up a notice on the office bulletin board offering the flat for rent when Max's hollow voice sounded behind me. "My wife Pol's looking for a place, too. You'd like her."

"Why should I like her if you don't?"

"She's a woman of character like you. And Josie's about the age of your daughter."

"Well, send her over and we'll try the girls out together."

I liked Pol. She took the flat, and to give her her own bedroom we put Josie on the second floor next to Caroline. Since they were only children they ought not to have got on with each other, but they chose to combine not their egotism but their loneliness and became good friends for a couple of years.

I liked Pol, who was a bit older than me, more cynical, though she shouldn't have been, since I was a newspaper reporter and she was a social worker. She'd travelled more than me, and the years with Max had hardened her to circumstance; the years with Jean-Louis had only frightened me. He was an art director and his world was nothing when it wasn't glamorous. I wasn't good at glamour and I was glad to get out of it.

We lived like college room-mates, keeping each other company, keeping out of each other's hair as well. We didn't get involved in food issues, Pol paid her rent on time, we kept a timetable that left the girls covered and ourselves free more than either of us had been while we were married, and I look on Pol's first years as some of the best times we've had in this house.

We didn't agree on everything, and it showed in the men we trailed home (hiding large pairs of boots in order not to alarm the girls) during the busy, sexy seventies when everyone our age was loose and hunting. She picked up Central Europeans who looked vaguely as if they were in Canada feeding up for the next revolution somewhere else. I mothered rather innocent young men: I was a kind of transition between home and the big wide world. I told myself I was preparing for the change in values that Caroline's teen-age years would evince.

It wasn't always perfect. She had to forgive me for using tinned soup and peanut butter. I had to live with the smell of the earthy messes of roots and leaves she cooked. She grew leeks in the front flower bed which wouldn't have been a sin if one of the neighbours hadn't reported it to the housing inspector, who insisted on also coming in, and finding many expensive flaws in the house. I called her Central Europeans by the wrong names, until I decided to call them all Max and to tell them I was crazy.

I did small jobs on whatever newspapers were giving out work, suburban or urban. I never was ambitious. She quarrelled with her supervisors, borrowed money from someone, and went back to school. When Jean-Louis told me to raise her rent to cover the new wiring, I didn't have the heart.

But I did do something else. I met my friend Heather in the supermarket one day, and when she told me her new job was finding rooms for ex-mental patients, I told her I had an empty room on the second floor. That was how we got Tom.

I thought he was fine. His social worker told me he was a bit withdrawn, had no psychoses, only problems about keeping appointments and facing the world. He certainly, she said, would be no threat to the girls.

He was tall, and very pale and thin, like a piece of bleached horseradish. He was on drugs, which made him immobile and quiet. Caroline wasn't afraid of him; I guess Pol and Josie were away on some kind of holiday when I agreed to take him.

They came in late one night and there was no chance to tell them about him; not that I remember, anyway. Next morning he came down, walking stiffly and slowly like an automaton and I said, "Pol, this is Tom. I've rented him the back room."

She looked up at him. I could tell she didn't like what she saw. "Where did you get him?" she asked.

"I'll tell you later."

He looked at her. Then he hung his head and shuffled out the door.

"That friend of yours who finds places for patients, huh?"

"Yes, but he's very nice. And it's going to pay for the wiring."

"Gwen, you idiot! The girls! The girls!"

"He's non-violent. He's got some kind of terrible background, but there's no psychosis. He just can't make decisions."

"I don't like him."

"Well, why not?"

"I've been in the work for years, darn it. I should know. You're so innocent about people. He's going to be nothing but a problem."

"He will be if you're negative."

"Listen, I wanted to live in a nice house, not a zoo."

"Your prejudices are showing."

"Well, I'll tuck them away for now. But you just wait, Gwen Tennyson, just you wait."

She always called me Gwen Tennyson when she thought I was being sentimental.

She was right, but not for good reasons. It wasn't the presence of Tom that changed things, it was Pol's attitude to Tom that changed things. The little girls got along with him fine, asked him to play Monopoly and Masterpiece with them, shared their television programs. But Pol had a kind of prurience that showed, and that shook me. "What does he do when he's bad?" she asked.

I replied reluctantly that I'd been told that when he lost his grip he forgot to put his clothes on.

"For God's sake, Gwen."

"Well, he hasn't yet."

But I was worried about him. Whenever he saw Pol he drew into some corner of himself that was very far away.

And I watched her after that, liked her less. I felt that the way she stared at him was wrong; I felt she was expecting him to go mad again, and that he was weak and willing enough to offer her his madness. And I knew by the way she had begun to complain about my housekeeping, my fading crowd of young men, the neighbourhood, that she was annoyed to have to share the house with him. I wondered about Max and his drinking, though Max had a nature that had been dedicated to self-destruction from childhood, I knew. Still, there was something about Pol: she could make me misbehave, and she could get at Tom.

"It's my house, Pol," I said a lot of times.

One Saturday morning Tom said he wasn't feeling very well. "I got scared of Pol," he said.

"You have to toughen up, Tom. There'll always be people who dislike your background."

He went out, then, and from the front window I watched him trying to get up the courage to cross the road, putting a foot out again and again and again and withdrawing it. Josie looked at him and sighed, "I wish Mum liked him. He's really nice, isn't he?"

"I wish he liked himself."

Pol was going out with a gaunt man from Central Europe who liked to come and cook extraordinary goulashes in the big downstairs kitchen and didn't clean up very well afterwards. When I taxed her with this, she said, "Well, you never use anything but a can opener. Why don't you move upstairs."

"Pol, it's my house."

Soon afterwards, I came home to find the police at the door and Pol screaming at Tom, who had no clothes on. I was pleased that the police were nice to him. "We'll take him to the hospital," they said. "Don't worry, ma'am." The little girls seemed unwounded, unoffended.

"Didn't I tell you," Pol said. "Now we can clean his room out and Max can live there."

"I don't want Max to live there."

"Why not, he's an old friend, isn't he?"

"You mean Max-Max, not your boyfriend?"

"Max, my ex-husband, Josie's benighted father. He's looking for a place."

"I don't want him. He's a drunk."

"How come you can have mental patients and not drunks? Josie needs her father."

"Pol, it's my house."

He came around and had a go at me. "Gwennie, I need to be near the kid."

"Max, I don't care if you're employed or unemployed, I don't want to live with you."

"What's wrong with me? We've been buddies, Gwen, buddies."

"You take too much joy in getting arrested. You drink too much."

"Well, you like a drink, too."

"I don't want you around, Max. You'll make trouble. I mean Pol has the odd friend, and it'll be hard to take."

"Listen, I have the odd friend too, it won't mean a thing."

I saw the house stacked up with bodies, and I said firmly and loudly again, "It's my house, no."

The upshot of this was that Pol took offence and dragged Josie out to an apartment in High Park where there was room for both Max and her lover. Then I took Josie back for a month while Pol recovered from the beating Max had administered because of the lover. I repainted the flat and rented it to library school students, and drove Josie and Pol to the airport to fly to England where Pol was to pursue her graduate studies. The seventies were over, and although Josie and Caroline clutched each other and cried at parting, Pol and I did not.

Then things changed. Caroline started high school and showed ominous signs of growing up on me. My young lovers grew up, too, and went off with girls their own age. My suburban newspapers folded one by one. I thought about a new career and decided that I was an ideal employee: I wanted an old-fashioned office job as dogsbody and telephone-answerer and mum.

I found one when an antique dealer on Queen Street advertised for a "universal aunt."

We've had our differences, Tibor and I. He doesn't admire pine furniture and he can't stand crazy quilts. He's critical of my attitude to furniture polishing. He thinks my bookkeeping is funny. On the other hand he likes my muscles, and the way

I always know where things are (that's after years of "Hey, Mum, where's my . . .?"). He likes the way I get to the store on time, always ask him before I name a price, and treat customers with respect.

After my downy youngsters, Tibor is a delight. He is ten years older than I am and has been through hell and high water in terms of wars and revolutions, which he won't talk about, he calls himself an Austro-Hungarian and if that's what he wants to be it's all right with me. He's a good cook.

Mindful of Pol and her root-cookers, I asked him when I first went to work for him what his politics were. I explained that if this was a cell or something, I didn't want to be in it. "If it's a cell, daughter," he said, "I'm a monk."

He isn't one.

He came to the house first because I said I might have room to store a couple of Empire sofas for him. He and Caroline took to each other at once. "He's just not like Dad," she said. "Not one bit. So I don't have to compare them, and that makes it easy," she told me.

Slowly, he began replacing my Salvation Army furniture (Jean-Louis had taken most of the smart stuff, and I'd never earned enough or cared enough to replace it) with his antiques. Then he decided he'd better move into the house to take care of it. He rented his flat above the store to the young man who does his gilding and bookbinding.

Some mornings I wake up beside him and pinch myself because I'm so happy. Then he says, "Don't pinch yourself. I'm here, and you're about to go downstairs and make tea. If we put that little Bokhara down, the bedroom will be warmer. I'm going to Sotheby's today, some new fool is getting rid of grandmother's Chippendale to replace it with distressed beech cut to look like pine and I don't think Rotenberg's going to bid on it. And I know a man who has just killed a goose: we shall eat tonight."

Off he goes, off I go. Sometimes we meet for lunch in the neighbourhood, and once in one of the new, smart places that make us feel very old and dignified and worldly wise, we were

waited on by Tom, who was happy to see me. When I explained that he had lived in the house, Tibor said, "Well, why
don't you invite him back now he's on lithium; if we rent a
room we'll eat better than ever."

So he did come back. He's fine, now. He can make decisions, he remembers to take his medication. He gets on with
Caroline, and the house, which is very large, feels full and
happy.

Happiness is a funny thing, like unpolluted air: you forget
what it was like when it's gone. It's transparent and somehow
silent.

A while ago, about five o'clock, I was home getting some
potatoes ready for dinner because it was my turn to cook and
Tibor's to close the store. The front hall was full of cartons of
bric-a-brac from an auction, and when the doorbell rang I
also had to squeeze past a large Regency bookcase Tibor had
brought up from a sale in Boston. I peered through the glass
panelling, and there was Pol, fatter and older.

"Hey, hi, when did you get back from England?"

"I just got off the plane. I came straight here. How are you,
stranger?"

"I'm terrific. Where's Josie?"

"She's still there: Max's rich aunt is sending her to boarding school. Hey, what's all this, gone into the antique
business?"

"Sort of. Come on in and I'll tell you about it."

I got out a bottle of Tibor's Tokay and some crystal glasses
he had brought home (there were only five in the lot) and
poured us a drink. "Now," she said, "let down your hair.
But first, let me know where I'm going to sleep tonight."

Let down your hair, Rapunzel, I thought. Let down your
hair.

"There's a not-bad tourist home on Spadina."

"Ah, come on Gwen, aren't we friends? Weren't we
always? I'm just off a plane, you don't have to string me.
What's wrong?"

"There isn't a bed in the place, Pol. There's half the school library on the top floor and I've got someone living with me."

On cue, Tibor bounced in, beamed, sat down, shook hands, took a drink. Then Caroline came home. When she heard Tom on the stairs she put her hand over her mouth in dismay and rushed out to warn him. "Tom's back," I said to Pol. "He's fine now. He's on lithium. I don't think you should cohabit: you've never liked each other."

Pol shook her head. "Gosh, every time, I think, there's one person I like, she's perfect, we get on fine; then you go and do it again: fill up your house with goons and mental patients and right wing pricks."

"Right wing pricks?" asked Tibor.

"Where're you from, mister? What was your name in the States?"

"Pol . . ."

"Shut up, Gwen. You're so dumb you don't know this guy is . . . I'm at a loss for words."

"I remember you," Tibor said slowly. "You used to go about with that little Alvarez before he committed suicide. Unlike Gwennyth, you dealt in other people's politics."

"You mean to say you didn't?"

I felt the happiness not so much fading as swallowing itself. I said suddenly, "Pol, get out."

Tibor said. "Gwen, I didn't mean to go that far."

I could feel Tom vibrating on the step outside the door. He would need Caroline to help him cross the road. I said, "Listen, Pol, we get on fine when there's no one else around, when you can decide who comes in and out of this house. But it's not that kind of house any more."

"Are you saying it's *your* house again in that nauseating way?"

"It's not my house. Tibor bought it from Jean-Louis last year. Tell me about England. Josie didn't tell us whether you finished your degree or not."

But she stood up and backed away. "I don't like what

you've turned into. I'd rather pay for a room in a hotel than stay where I'm not welcome.''

"I'm sorry, Pol. But we can't have Tom upset when he's doing so well."

"Stop saying you're sorry. I'm going." She stormed out through the hall, banging into the big bookcase. If she'd had an umbrella she'd have put it through the glass in its doors. "Max is dead and you don't even care," she said. "I'm just off the plane, you turn me out . . .''

I let her go. Caroline watched her with narrowed brows. "She doesn't have any luggage," Caroline said.

"Max isn't dead."

Tom drifted into the living-room on a sigh. "I don't know why she upsets me," he said.

"She reminds you of someone," I said.

He thought. "Marjorie. My sister Marjorie. She used to tell Dad I'd wet the bed when she couldn't get what she wanted."

"It's just that there are people like that," I said. "Don't worry about her. They don't get power over you unless you let them."

"And she did run the house, Mum," Caroline put in. "You did everything she told you."

"I was a younger sister. Used to taking orders."

"Not completely," Tibor said with a laugh. Then he filled our two glasses again and raised his own to the light. "I congratulate you: you have developed at last a sense of evil. You are now grown up."

I see her sometimes on the street, now, but if she sees me she puts her head down and slouches angrily past. I don't know what makes her feel so shabbily treated when she is not allowed to rule; I feel that she is eaten by some old anger. I wish she'd do something about it. I wish she'd learn to share our happiness.

Because we are happy, Tibor and Tom and Caroline and I.

We're so happy that sometimes even Jean-Louis and his wife drop by for a drink and a piece of preserved goose and a joke, and we share this happiness with them carefully, spoon by spoon, in memory of other times when things were not so good.

Two Rosemary Road, Toronto

Two Rosemary Road, Toronto

Dear Betty Weller Kipling:

Thank you for your sympathetic letter of September 18 which I am now able to answer.

You are correct in the assumption that a death in the family causes a great upheaval, but after a period of obligatory confusion and mourning, we are now able to return to more-or-less normal life and do our homework, of which this letter is a sample.

Mary was indeed a wonderful person and after a marriage of twenty-four years I find myself bereft without her. We did, however, have ample warning that her death was near, hence time to prepare ourselves. I learned to cook, the children to look after themselves and each other and we had a number of sad practice sessions in doing without her when she was in hospital. She, in her turn, did her homework by working through the process of dying. It was not easy for her but she said that in the end it was easier to die because she had imagined the process and dealt with some of her fears. She no longer, I am pleased to say, imagined heaven as a large stone public school with St Peter as principal and herself the new student. In the end she found herself unable to imagine Eternity at all, but said that she understood why Goethe asked for more light. I found these discoveries hard to share, but when my own time comes I shall be richer for them. Neither of us being religiously inclined, we did not take seriously visions of a heaven full of harpists in togas. After all, there is, as you have stated, the problem of the Jews, and this is now a Jewish neighbourhood.

I am afraid I cannot agree with you that cancer is the disease of those who give up. Mary literally fought her disease over a period of twelve years. Although she did not resume her career (she was a secretary with the Iranian Oil Company when I met her in Persia), she did not appear to be bored or unhappy at home. She did a good deal of volunteer work once the children were launched into full-time school, delivering meals to the elderly, succouring other cancer patients, etc. and was devoted to her garden, I believe because she had grown up in rocky terrain where gardening was impossible. She was patient with the children and their many problems, and if she was unhappy she did not indicate that this was so: therefore I do not count myself responsible for her disease.

It may be true, as you state, that unhappiness causes one to be susceptible to cancer; if that is so, I am certainly breeding it now. However, I fail to see what one can do about another person's unstated unhappiness. I am an abstracted fellow and was a less than sociable husband; I might have mended my ways if my wife had told me to do so; it was my mother-in-law who held me in low estimation, however, and I was not married to her. I do not think Mary had given up at all; I think she had cancer, which is what she died of. I think it often made her feel like giving up. She was brave, and did not.

As for fighting the good fight, she and I did discuss techniques of visualization. She disliked the idea of sending white knights out from her thymus to conquer her cancer. "I don't want to be polluted by a bunch of Teutonic pencil box figures,'' she said to me once. She did, however, experiment with imagining Pac-man consuming her cancer cells. It didn't do much to hold off the night, but I suspect it helped her get to sleep.

I believe she had the best treatment available in North America, but who can tell? She might have done better to sit up to her neck in the mudbaths of Banff or wherever they are, or consume an enormous daily ration of papaya juice and liver, or . . . The cause of cancer is not yet known. If it is modern civilization, let me remind you that the disease pre-dates modern civilization. It seems to be on the rampage now and my own theory is that it is itself a survivor, where typhoid and tuberculosis have been eliminated by the medical knights. We need only a method, and then we will see what prevents us next from outliving Methuselah.

Thank you for your concern for my welfare, which I find relatively unimportant at the moment. I exist and that is enough. I do indeed remember you vividly. You sat beside me in Professor Parker's class and it was to me that you first an-nounced your astonishing decision to cause him to leave his wife and marry you. You were the first young woman I knew to succeed in such an enterprise and I am sorry the adventure made neither of you happy. Mrs Parker's bitterness was understandable, however.

I do not recollect that I was a rich young man, and I was certainly not a Jewish young man with a changed name when you first met me; I think you thought me Jewish because you thought me rich, a connection many people erroneously make. The fact was that my grandfather was what people call well off, and lived in this neighbourhood, and this house; he had many Jewish neighbours, but was the survivor of a con-servative and intolerant Gentile community. He was also old and mad. If I had more money at my disposal than some other students, and his car, it is because I lived alone with him and had power of attorney over what then seemed to be a large sum of money. I used his clubs, his symphony tickets, and his tailor. I ate in restaurants in order to avoid sharing with him the pap his housekeeper made him. If you remember the restaurants of Toronto then, you will recall they were not grand. I spent a great deal of my university time at Bowles's. When Mary as she said "took me over," I had the habits of a ninety-year-old man, which is why you found me remote. Had I been Jewish I would not have been able to go to his clubs, but I would not, either, have felt obliged to eat the dreadful food that was offered me in the restaurants I knew about.

I am still, probably, the remote and difficult (or was it "diffident" you wrote, I cannot decipher your scrawl) person you recall from university. I am not aware, however, that I took a vow to be faithful to Mary after her death, and if I meet any one her equal I shall be prepared to assuage my loneliness, remote and difficult and spoiled as I am. I have no intention of making off with any of my students: you probably provided an early cure for that. I shall, as Mary wished, see the children through school and university, providing as good a home as I can for them, marrying if and when I choose, but not in order to find a housekeeper: these can be hired.

In re-reading the above, I doubt that I have conveyed my entire disapproval of your missive. It is irritating to be shoved into a different religious group because of a misremembered university status; it is infuriating to be accused of being the agent of Mary's cancer, and to be asked personal questions about it.

If you have cancer yourself, go and do something about it. If you are looking for a husband, look elsewhere.

Meanwhile, led the dead past bury its own, as the Prophet says. If you are unhappy, I regret it, but I am outraged at the implication that your unhappiness is the equal of mine. Surely each of us is entitled to his own form of mourning. . . .

It was getting late, and the more he wrote the worse the letter got. He tore it up and moved to the night window and looked out at the October sleeping street. The trollop, he thought, the trollop, pleased at the antique word. I must have been a strange boy. She had enormous breasts that seemed to move around with a life of their own: a shirtful of serpents distracting one from the Nichomachean ethics. We all wanted her, Parker particularly, and much good she did him. She was clever, though, ought to have been above false logic, anti-semitism, foolish manipulative assertions about Mary. She ought to have grown into something beyond that. Perhaps she was desperate.

He stood staring at the damp, shining pavement, thinking of the look certain women students had, a chocolatey acquisitive glow. It was as if they wanted to eat his brains with a long-handled spoon, but very prettily. I never gave in, he thought, and Mary knew. I gave her that.

He thought a moment, scratched himself, fetched the letter out of the basket, unscrewed it, and laughed at his prickliness. Parker was the apple on the tree twenty-five years ago, God help him. Fancy, now she wants me, not the *père de famille*, but the lad in his grandfather's ulster. Nothing wrong with having a crack at it, he supposed. No morals, women, men.

Deep inside him stirred like the waving dark branch of the Rosensteins' copper beech across the road the first flickering desire to end his solitude. He turned his study light out without putting a name or indeed a neighbourhood to his mild and contented swelling.

Gemini, Gemino

Gemini, Gemino

He was a decent man, a fair husband, and a good writer. He knew that. He had seen these statements written in the newspapers and written on his heart.

And his wife lay weeping on the sand. His son Douglas was far away, on the crest of a small islanded rock, playing stout Cortez. The beach was very beautiful. Douglas and Joan descended to it on a rope through a hole in the bank, romantically. Because of his bad leg he had to walk down the road to a cut in the bank, then wade in the ice-cold water to meet them. As fair compensation, a fat seal came to meet him half way, sleekly rolling its fat bottom in the waves and seeming to wave its flippers at him every morning. They should have been happy.

He was full of guilt, but he was also angry. Murchison had been promising to lend them his cottage for years and they had looked forward to this expedition with appetite. They were as far east in the country as you could go, there was nothing between them and Spain. The east coast always impressed him, though he seldom saw it in winter. In spite of its natural depression, it was salt and dramatic and bracing; it stimulated him as the more mysterious and tropical west could not. He had planned that this would be his perfect summer, and there she was, graceless, in a heap on the sand, a bottom larger than the seal's advanced to the maritime air, weeping.

And he had done it.

They had been married for a good fifteen years, since his first novel came out. She knew that there would be difficulties marrying someone as essentially solitary and moody as a writer, but as she was a quiet person herself — an accountant by trade — she had said she enjoyed his quiet life, and he thought that she meant it. He was paid very little for his books, which were his best work, and fairly well for radio programs, which he enjoyed doing; and very well for television material, which he was bad at. She was well paid, and subsidized his avoidance of the worst kind of hackwork. They had only Douglas, who was ten, a rather tentative child, but an easy and intelligent one.

Subjects for novels, which at their best are products of one's interior life, did not come to him easily. His were considered good in a quiet way. They were never best sellers, but he was a thoughtful, workmanlike writer and had a small, solid following and a good reputation in the universities. He was treated seriously in the most pleasant way when a book came out, though none had appeared for three years.

When people asked Joan if it wasn't difficult being married to a writer, she always replied, ''But you see, I get to read the books first!'' and smiled radiantly. But their current trouble had come from this, and he did not know what to do. He felt like packing her up and lugging her back to town. How could he build new castles in this marvellous air if she was to lie there, being dreary, sobbing at him, embarrassing poor Douglas?

She was a good wife, a loyal wife, somewhat utilitarian in appearance and approach, inclined to the practical rather than the aesthetic, but there for him, never a flirt. The exotic was an element in their lives he had to supply for himself; but he, because of his bad leg, and the consequent depressions and distortions and misprisions of self-image, knew how to do that himself. He cooked up a storm when he felt like it and had put himself in charge of decorating their house in such a way that it had both comfort and visual magic. He brought interesting people home. She, on the other hand, had a talent for bringing the best out in them, asking their stories, cultivating them in a motherly sort of way, making them feel at home. They were, it was said, an ideal combination. Not *arty*. You could trust the Lewises, and enjoy them. He was a bit temperamental, apt to take offence, but he'd had polio as a child, you know. Pretty solid writer, too, they said about him, though on the dull side. They were waiting for him to develop an idea with a little more passion to it. There was a feeling that he had not yet put all of himself on the page.

He had that feeling too; there was some reserve in him that he had not been able to break through up until now.

But he had just finished a novel that he was proud of, one dealing with material belonging to Joan's life, material she had given him permission to use. It had taken him two years to get it right, focus on the important elements and arrange the proportions. The final draft had come easily and had seemed to him so essentially right that it could not fail to please both scholarly readers, whom he valued, and the public, whom he needed. He had given it to her to read with the most intense pride: and then this had happened.

The blue sea lapped against the red, shaly shore. The sun was approaching the zenith. Soon they would scrabble back up to the cottage for a lunch of beans and bologna. Meanwhile Joan lay in a kind of dug-out she had made, dozing and waking only to weep. "I'll get it out of my system," she said, "I really will."

It's hell being decent, he thought. We should yell at each other.

He had gone to a psychiatrist for years, finding his interior solitude and his solitary work habits too much to bear; he had finally accepted the fact that he was a brooder, it was part of his nature and part of his trade. He saved his emotions for the printed page. He could not yell, though today he was tempted to kick her. It took the joy out of Dougie's holiday, after all. And his own.

He saw Douglas wave from the big rock. Anxiously, never understanding that other people were more agile than he was, for when he lost the use of his right leg the rest of the world had lost theirs too, he watched him climb down the cliff, wade through the freezing water — that it was too cold to swim made it easier to supervise the child, who was an otter — and run towards him. Hunger was separating him from his kingdom.

He spoke to Joan. "Doug's coming. We'd better go up for lunch."

She sat up at once, stretched, and staggered to the water, where she cooled her swollen face. Her figure was lumpy and she walked apologetically in the bathing-suit now. She belonged to a generation of women who had been well fed on meat and potatoes and some of their bodies could not forget this.

"I'm sorry," she sighed, as she led the climb up the bank — he could negotiate the upward path with his stick, not the downward — "I'm sorry. I'm sorry."

"It's okay, Mum," Douglas said. "I had a neat time. I think I saw a puffin. Can we go back to the lagoon to look for the avocets this afternoon?"

"Sure," they both said, "sure."

What was sure in their lives was that they would try to give him everything. If he grew up and said, "But I wanted joy," they would have to explain that parents could not always supply that.

His parents had been intellectuals, cold and remote. He was a late child, and his mother had been unsure of how to treat him. "I never knew whether to pick you up or not," she

had told him. "So I just left you there. You were all right as soon as you learned to read, but you must have been lonely."
He was.

She, on the other hand had grown up in a big family. Three boys and then two daughters had been born to an army supply officer. His meagre salary had not been much increased when he turned schoolteacher after the war, but she had grown up in a cheerful knot of children, or so it appeared. She and her sister were twins. The sister, blinded by measles at three, had been raised partly at the School for the Blind in Brantford, and died there at the age of twelve. His novel was about a man who fell in love with the Joan of a pair of twins, and then became attracted to the blind Elspeth, who had not died at the age of twelve. He had based it on all her stories, which were many and supremely interesting to him, and talks he had had with his psychiatrist about the gestalt of such a situation. There were, however, points that he had missed. The novel had enraged her and then brought on some kind of breakdown.

They saved their gourmandising for the evenings on the island; lunched on boiled vegetables and bologna and white bread from the local store. Remote islands are not rich in summer's fare. Towards evening he would drive to the docks to see what the fishermen had brought in, and if they were lucky they would find berries near the lagoon as well as avocets this afternoon. No doubt Joan would find a little inlet where she could sit and cry, but he and Douglas would hunt for walrus teeth and pretend that there were also Viking artifacts in wait for them.

"Do you remember Linda who lived in our basement to baby-sit the year you were writer-in-residence and away?" Joan asked. "I'm like her. She was trying to do a primal scream, which was a kind of therapy, Douglas, that everyone was indulging in then. You had to get your early feelings out. I seem to be suffering from some kind of awful grief."

He had urged her to go to a psychiatrist, but she said she

thought it was too late. And anyway all her friends who had gone to psychiatrists had left their husbands, and she didn't want to, if he didn't mind.

In a way, he recognized, he did mind. She was spoiling his holiday.

The island they were on was a mixture of French and English, though the English were departing now that it was officially part of Quebec. It had long been a fiefdom of an English family which was so exigent about land rent that neither population was able to prosper. But now things were desperate: the herring were moving away or fished out and none of the makework projects the provincial government had invented except tourism had brought any income. The people had too long lived alone to enjoy tourism much; they felt invaded and often showed it. Still, there were a few friendly souls, and Lewis's French was good, he got along.

Thus it was that that afternoon, driving a short way down to the lagoon beach, where the water was warm enough for Douglas to swim, he was able to stop and give directions to a van full of Quebecois. In return, they said they were starting an adventure campground for boys Douglas's age, and invited him to visit. He shifted shyly in his seat, but the sight of other boys' faces in the back of the van obviously cheered him. He had learned a little French at school. "J'ai un snor-kell," he said, and they waved at him wildly.

So the next day they left him there, snorkel and birdbook, rather pleased to be rid of him — evenings were long when the mosquitoes came out like dive-bombers at six o'clock and they were tired of playing "The Minister's Cat" — and decided to talk to each other.

"Look," he said, "you said I could. But I won't publish it if you don't want. But you have to tell me why."

The accountant in her came out. "You can't throw away two years' work. And it's good."

"I know it's good. That's why I'm desperate. But if it has this effect on you now, what will happen if it comes out? You've got to go and see someone."

"I don't think I need to. I just have to get over this bad space. Anyway, you can be my psychiatrist, you've gone to Thing for long enough, you know all about it." His supposed intimacy with Dr Thibault was a sore point with her, she was afraid he complained about her, that Dr Thibault knew more about her than she did herself. Which might, in the circumstances, now be true.

"It's just," she said, "that being confronted by it all from your point of view is such a shock. And it seems so romantic. You know I've always hated novels about twins: Iris Murdoch's, and that thing of Patrick White's. You novelists are too darn romantic, you're always doing ESP twins, and it's not that way at all, at least it wasn't with Elspeth. In a way we weren't close at all. I never knew what she was thinking. And damn it all, you rub my nose in it."

Family, he thought, never understands fiction. Every writer knows that, and has to tough it out, or else wait until they're dead to use the material. There's no way around hurting them. And she's not a good reader, she's too practical, a thing has to be as plotted as Trollope before she can enjoy it. "I've told you a thousand times," he said. "I start from myself, or myself and you, as the case is here, and then in draft after draft the characters become more and more themselves, and move in their own direction. Russell Frye is not Lawrence Lewis any more than the Page twins are you and Elspeth."

"But you can't blame me for reading it from my point of view. And there's that smarmy devotion between them, Larry, it's as terrible as a Harlequin romance."

"You talk about Elspeth that way. All of you in your family. There's an odour of sanctity when her name is mentioned. She must have been wonderful."

Joan sighed and slouched. "She was pretty. She had yellow ringlets, like Shirley Temple. I was the one with the dark straight hair and the cast in my eye. I hated her. I've told you and told you. She was blind."

He was fourteen when he came down with polio. He had

been formed as a healthy child and turned into a maimed adolescent. Still, he was uncomfortable with this disclosure of Elspeth's handicap; it put Joan in a strange position.

This was as far as they ever got in their talks. "I hated her."

Inside himself he felt the gloom of ambivalence. To be fair to her, he must rewrite the book to turn the hero more positively towards the Joan-figure, or else understand and emphasize the hate, and either way the book, he thought, would be ruined. Though it might be more honest. But that was what they complained of in his work, its dull honesty.

And he had grown enamoured of the Elspeth figure. Any man married to a brunette, he supposed, will eventually romanticize a blonde. Perhaps it even worked vice-versa.

They were sitting out on a pair of tedious plastic lawn chairs in front of the cottage. They could not even see the sea. "I hated her and you've shown me why I hated her. Why shouldn't I cry? I hate my hate. I feel guilty for my hate. She was blonde, she had curly hair, she was handicapped and pretty. The boys all adored her. Nobody paid any attention to me. 'Oh, Joan can manage,' everyone said, and I must say that's just what I learned. Is it my fault I've never learned to manage that? That somehow they turned me into a big, utilitarian . . . horse?

"We were twins and everyone is sentimental about twins. In death they were not divided, that sort of thing. When she went to the school in Brantford Mother used to take me there. She was supposed to keep in contact with her twin sister. But I was scared at the school, it was in the middle of a big wood and we had to walk through it from the bus stop — we didn't have a car then, no schoolteacher with five kids had a car — and I was only little, I thought that stumps were skunks and very dangerous. And Mother would put me down to sit on a stump while she pushed Elspeth on the swings in the playground. I couldn't go on the swings: I was sighted. There were a lot of things you couldn't do if you were sighted, like attract Mother's attention.

"Some of the teachers understood, and one of them used to talk to me sometimes. When she left, I wouldn't go there any more. I had tantrums whenever they mentioned the bus to Brantford. And when Elspeth came home for holidays I stopped being the only girl and became, well, the drudge. Everything stopped so everyone could be good to Elspeth. I wanted to shove her off the edge of the earth."

"From the other stories you've told me, surely not all the time."

"Oh, sometimes when they left us alone together we got on. After the first few visits. At first she'd pinch me so I'd cry; then she'd say I'd hit her: the kind of thing ordinary siblings do, which you wouldn't know about, being an only child. But we got that evened out, Mother wasn't dumb, and sometimes we did have fun together. She had a wonderful imagination, and made up stories, I told you that. I suppose it's what attracted me to you. But what's coming out now is a terrible feeling, like a barbed worm inside me, a kind of old cancer. All that jealousy, all that disappointment, all that hate. She was a fairy child, and they made so much of her."

"But you had your talents, too; your practicalities, your abilities."

"But I never felt I developed them alone. If she was beautiful, I had to be ugly. If she got attention, I had to be self-effacing. I picked my complexion off when I was a teenager just to establish a separate personality. That's when I should have gone to a psychiatrist, only of course there were hardly any then. And then of course there was the fact that she died. What turned her to marble. You've put her down, the romantic Elspeth. The real Elspeth once tried to scratch my eyes out and by God I nearly let her; it took me a minute to realize that if I hid she couldn't find me, so I got away. Twins are vicious, Larry. All you writers, I don't know, you invent a kind of companion to take your solitude away, but you don't know what it's like to be dogged by one.

"I'm being bad, now. I'm spoiling your holiday. But you

see what you've done to me: you've chosen my sister. You can't expect me to put up with that! You might as well be having an affair. And I'm too old and ugly to replace you. Let's just hope Dougie gets on with these boys, and you can have a few days' beachcombing and I can get over my sulks. But you've hurt me, and I don't know what to do with the book.''

''I'll throw it out.''

''You damn well won't. You know you're not going to, too.''

He knew that.

On the beach alone the next day he found himself hating her hectoring, lecturing voice, her moral superiority. The way she never got drunk, never lost control, never stopped watching him, mothering him: it was even annoying when she was shaking, red-eyed. At the end of the summer he could tell Dr Thibault about it and relieve his feelings.

Douglas's French gave out on the third day, and he refused to return to the adventure camp. Lewis took him to the lagoon for the day. They worked on their bird lists. He did not ask where Joan went.

They flew away from the islands with the wrong kind of regret a few days later.

She went back to work, and he launched into the canning season. He loved the Keatsian richness of the harvest, and made chili sauces and pickles and chutneys to spice the winter, preserves from their own two fruit trees for morning toast. It made him feel rich and successful, and he was no longer the only man of his acquaintance who made such things. He was happy.

She was not. She sprained her ankle the first week back at work, and walked as lamely as he did. It put her in a bad temper, as did the heat, and the wasps that invaded the kitchen. She was fatter, too, and disgruntled when another writer received major attention in the morning paper. ''You've got to get that book out.''

''I can't figure out what to do.''

"Maybe the dear Thibault will help you when he comes back."

"If you take that attitude, you deserve what you get."

"Oh, I've always deserved what I've got," she said, and the look she gave him was unpleasant. Her long toenails ripped him in bed that night.

He and Thibault discussed parallels and he came away gloomy. Perhaps she had hated him all along; found in him another twin to assault in the womb.

His agent phoned, anxious to see whether there was work to present to a publisher. He said he couldn't make up his mind about it and weakly consented to let her decide what to do. She was an excellent marketer, but her taste was not always literary. He felt even worse when he had put the decision in her hands.

"It's cheap sensationalist crap," Joan said. "They'll offer you a lot of money, just you wait."

They did.

Joan did the driving and that weekend when they were invited north, she ran them off the edge of the road. Thibault had warned that he might have provoked this kind of crisis. She had been in some kind of control, however, since they ran into a wooden fence rather than a ditch or a tree. But she frightened them badly, and even Douglas knew that she had at some level done it on purpose. "You can't sell me," she muttered in the hospital emergency department while their cuts and bruises were bound, "damn it all, Larry, you can't sell me. You can hit me, you can leave me, but you can't sell me." He had cut that deep.

He withdrew the book and took on a television project. She in turn agreed to see someone at the Clarke Institute. Douglas had a sickly winter and began to read the Tolkien books. They lived that winter like sleepwalkers.

He had done the decent thing, but he was not happy, and he did not want even to talk to Thibault about it. Art and morality seemed too big a topic for a mere psychiatrist.

"Someone has killed someone," Thibault at last remarked, "that's what you seem to feel. Are you accusing her of killing her sister?"

He didn't want to think about it. It was too complex for him. She had made him feel indecent about his book.

And she had her own Thibault to talk to, and was more remote. "I know," she said, "that I'm leaving you completely open to a mid-life crisis: you risk meeting someone else. But in this I have to go my own way, you can see that, aren't you enough of an artist?" Some women, he thought, are too intelligent.

January and February were always his good months; the dark short days leading to the long dark nights carried their own intense silence and urged him to break it on paper. He sat down with the novel and the scales fell from his eyes. He started on the first page and began again. He put all his hate in it, and all the new things he knew, and his hate was eloquent and his new knowledge was true. He sent it away without showing it to her.

She began the long process of unbending like a drenched flower after a storm. The person she talked to was young and handsome and she began to hold herself straight, lose weight, and dress well. Lewis was jealous, though he knew the psychiatrist was honest and supplied, as Thibault did to him, an attention that a weary spouse has run out of. He began to compete with the man, spend a little money on himself. She was spending, too, and for the first time their menage lost its frugality. 'If you sell me," she said, "sell me well."

Douglas began to play Dungeons and Dragons.

The book's very intensity brought it a small, Canadian and respectable kind of fame. It earned prestigious reviews in England but was too low-key for the Americans. Joan took up yoga and left him alone more than ever. He committed untold extravagances with the Garden Club catalogue, refused to appear on psychological panels about twins, and lived in fear and hope of meeting a beautiful fair woman who was blind.

Other books by William Barrett

THE TRUANTS
ILLUSION OF TECHNIQUE
IRRATIONAL MAN